Sue Limb first started writing as a child. There was no TV in the house until she was fourteen, so writing stories was a way of creating fantasy adventures. After studying English Literature at university, Sue tried her hand at teaching English and Drama. When she finally gave up being a teacher, she started writing for teenage magazines instead.

Sue has written over twenty books for people of all ages, and also produced newspaper columns, TV series and radio comedy. Being a radio broadcaster is one of her favourite things because you don't have to look your best!

Betsy, Sue's nineteen-year-old daughter, is her greatest inspiration. Sue lives in Gloucestershire, dividing her time between her partner Steve's farm and her own little cottage, which is ever so slightly haunted.

You can find out more about Sue at her website: www.suelimb.com

*For Ben and Polly Dunbar*

ORCHARD BOOKS
96 Leonard Street, London EC2A 4XD
*Orchard Books Australia*
32/45-51 Huntley Street, Alexandria, NSW 2015
ISBN 1 84362 614 4
First published in Great Britain as *China Lee* in 1987
First published in paperback by Lions in 1989
This edition first published in 2004
Text © Sue Limb 1987, 2004
The rights of Sue Limb to be identified as the author of
this work has been asserted by her in accordance with
the Copyright, Designs and Patents Act, 1988.
A CIP catalogue record for this book is available from
the British Library.
1 3 5 7 9 10 8 6 4 2 (paperback)
Printed in Great Britain

# You're Amazing Mr Jupiter

## Sue Limb

ORCHARD BOOKS

# 1

China Lee looked out of her bedroom window across the city roofs, and grinned to herself. Her big sister Rose scowled into the mirror.

"Oh, my nose!" sighed Rose. "I think it's grown since yesterday! If it gets much longer it'll touch my chin!"

"You're never satisfied, Rose," China said, staring through the spires and skyscrapers.

"Well, I suppose it could be worse." Rose slapped on another layer of make-up. "I'm glad I haven't got your snub nose. On a clear day I can practically see your brains."

"At least I *have* brains, Rose," said China. "Hey! There's a rainbow! I can see where it ends! That's supposed to be where the pot of gold is buried."

"Where does it end?"

"Over there – by the bank."

"Surprise, surprise. It's all stupid superstition anyway," snapped Rose, rolling mascara on to her eyelashes.

"You're useless, Rose!" said China. "You don't believe in anything. You don't believe in haunted houses – you don't believe in aliens – you don't even believe in God."

"At least I believe in keeping the bedroom tidy. There was a bus ticket in my moisturiser today. You've been messing about with my things again, China."

"I have not!" yelled China. "The dog knocked it over, and the lid came off, that's all. I put the lid back on again – what more do you want?"

"That dog isn't supposed to come in our bedroom anyway. Mum says so. He leaves hairs everywhere."

"Well, so do you. He can't help it. And you'd soon change your tune if we had burglars and he chased them off."

"We'd never have burglars," sighed Rose. 'There's nothing in this house that anyone would ever want to steal."

"Yes, there is!" China said. "There's my silver cup

I won for running last year – and my secret diary and my stickers."

"Wow!" said Rose, covering her lips with gloss. "Your secret diary and your stickers! Don't tell Sonny Sangster the Gangster. He'll die of excitement."

China looked at all her things. She could see quite a lot of them at once, because she never put anything away. Her clothes, both the clean ones and the dirty ones, were jumbled together in a huge pile. It looked as if several people had fainted, all in a heap. At the bottom of the heap, a pair of limp blue legs stuck out to show where her jeans were. They looked as if their legs were broken. China felt sorry for her clothes, all of a sudden. She started picking them up and folding them away.

But it was even worse to think of any of her things being stolen. The sticker book containing China's vast collection of sparklies and cute animals. The secret diary, in which China wrote all her private stuff. It had a purple cover with the stars and moon shimmering in silver paper. China had cut them out and stuck them on by candlelight, whilst she whispered a special spell. She imagined the diary and the sticker book disappearing into a burglar's sack, the stars and moon vanishing into the dark.

"Oh Rose, Rose!" she sobbed. "If a burglar stole my secret diary and my stickers, I think I'd die!"

"You big softy!" said Rose, grinning. "Here – give me a hug. Not too hard, though – you'll smudge my make-up." For two sisters who hated each other so much, they managed quite a few hugs.

"Now, don't worry," whispered Rose. "If a burglar comes, I'll scare him off."

"Yes," said China, starting up at Rose's mascara, eye shadow and lip gloss. "He'll take one look at all that make-up and think you're a witch doctor!"

"You pig, China!" Rose screamed and gave her a mighty push. She was amazingly strong for somebody on so many diets. China flew backwards and landed on the pile of clothes.

"I'll get you!" yelled China, grabbing her Squirt-Some-Dirt Aerosol Fun can, left over from last year's Halloween.

"Eeeeeek!" shrieked Rose.

But then, from downstairs, came a voice which stopped them in their tracks.

"China! Rose! Cut it out! Come down here and help me with the dinner or you'll both be in big trouble!"

It was a big bass voice. Was their mum, perhaps, a champion weight-lifter? No, no. This was their dad. And China and Rose had a very special dad. He'd been, well, redesigned.

## 2

Mr Lee had lost his job and it was really hard to find a new one. At first, he sat and cursed at the TV or threw slippers at the dog. Then, one day, he got interested in cooking. It was the day China's mum said, "I won't be home till late, John – could you make the dinner?"

She was just starting up in business, in partnership with her brother, (China's uncle Tony, famous for his martial arts high kicks. He was the only one of China's uncles who regularly switched the light off with his big toe.) They were going to run a cybercafé in town.

Every day, China's mum went off to the soon-to-be-opened Surfshack.com. Actually, it was very small – about the size of an average garage. She was cleaning the place up and painting it, ready for the Grand Opening. So all of a sudden, she wasn't at home so much any more. And dinner somehow didn't get cooked. But wait! China's dad had discovered a book called Great Dishes of World Cookery.

"Aha!" he had said. "Listen to this! *Gugelhupf!* That's an Austrian cake! And *kisyeli* – that's a Russian pudding. And *thetchouka!*"

"Bless you, Dad," China had said. And tonight she could smell something really good.

"What's for dinner, Dad?"

"Beef Carbo-something-or-other. It's from Argentina."

"But Dad!" said Rose. "I told you – I'm a vegetarian."

"Come on, Rose. I can't make a separate dinner just for you."

"I don't think it's right to kill animals to eat."

"Well," said Dad, "if the Good Lord didn't want us to eat beef, why did he put all those cows on the earth?"

"He didn't put anything anywhere," said Rose. "They just evolved."

"They did what?"

11

"Evolved. You know – developed. All the animals did."

"Rose doesn't believe in God," said China. "But there must be a God, mustn't there? He made the world – it says so in the bible."

"No, he didn't!" argued Rose. "It was a Big Bang in space. That's where the earth came from, and all the other planets."

"There'll be a Big Bang round here unless I get some help in a minute," warned Dad.

Rose and China went to the cupboard and got out the plates and knives.

"If there isn't a God," China went on, "how come there's miracles and rainbows and things?"

"If there is a God," Rose asked, "how come there's fires and diseases and innocent people getting hurt in earthquakes and stuff?"

China thought about that for a minute. Was Rose right, after all? China was sure there must be some kind of God, somewhere. If there wasn't, she'd certainly wasted a lot of time talking to him over the years.

"Oh no! The beef's burnt," said Dad. "Now, why would God go and let me do a thing like that?"

The door slammed, and China's mum staggered in and crumpled up on the sofa like a puppet whose strings have snapped.

"My goodness!" she gasped. "I'm exhausted! That smells great, though, John – what is it?"

"Carbonado of dead cow," said Rose. "And God burnt it."

"Only round the edges!" China said. "It's OK, really, Dad. Come on, Mum! Let's eat! I'm absolutely starving!"

After dinner, the doorbell rang. Rose went bright red, even through the layers of make-up, and ran off to answer it.

"Nick," said China, and scowled. Nick was Rose's boyfriend. He never stopped smiling and telling jokes, but that made China hate him even more.

"Hi, kid,' he said, strolling in and pulling her hair. "Hello, Mr Lee, Mrs Lee – how's the cybercafe?" China's parents made him sit down, gave him coffee, and laughed at his jokes, but China felt herself starting to snarl, deep down inside, like a bad-tempered dog.

"Rose was just telling me about evolution, Nick," said Mr Lee. "What do you think? Did we all change from apes into human beings millions of years ago?"

Nick looked hard at China, and cocked his head on one side.

"Apes? Yeah, I think so, Mr Lee. Only with some of us maybe it wasn't quite so long ago…eh, China?"

"Ha, ha – very funny," said China, and jumped down from the table. "Mum, I have to go out."

"Where?"

"It's for a school project. We're going to visit old people and help them wash the dishes and things."

"You could start by helping us old people wash ours," said Dad.

"Oh, no, Dad. I mean *really* old people. I've got to visit somebody called Mr Jupiter. He lives in Lordship Road. Here's the address."

"Is this all properly organised?" asked Mum.

"Of course it is, Mum. I brought a letter home from school two weeks ago. You remember! Mrs Edwards organised it. And Mr Jupiter is expecting me."

"OK, OK," sighed Mum. "But be home before dark. And you'd better take Staff with you. He needs some exercise."

"C'mon, Staff!" called China, grabbing her jacket. A black shape bounded out from under the table. Staff was China's dog. He was a Staffordshire Bull Terrier. He had teeth like a shark, and when he got angry, he foamed at the mouth. If anybody ever tried to harm China, Staff would certainly make hamburgers out of them. So her parents reckoned she was pretty safe.

Staff and China banged out of the house and ran the first hundred yards to celebrate being out. It was a wonderful evening. The sun was warm on the dusty chestnut trees. The traffic hummed in the distance.

Great evening, God, thought China. And thanks for the dinner, too. I'm sorry I stuck the chewing gum on the bottom of my bed. And please make Mr Jupiter really, really nice.

Was God listening? You never can tell.

# 3

Mr Jupiter's house was old and tall, and tottering. It looked quite creepy. The door had once been painted yellow, but it was all flaking and blistering now. The curtains were torn and dirty. China felt quite nervous as she rang the bell.

"Please, God, make him not too weird," she prayed. She heard someone shuffling along inside the hall. It sounded as if he had webbed feet – flop, flop, flop. Then the door rattled and it inched open with a creak.

A beard peeped out at her. Above the beard were two friendly but slightly frightened brown eyes.

"Who's there?" croaked a wobbly voice.

China realised he was more frightened than she was. She felt a lot better.

"Mr Jupiter?" she asked. "I'm China Lee. I've

come to visit you – you know, for my school project!"

"Ah, yes! Come in, come in!" Mr Jupiter stood aside for her to go into the house. He even held his beard back politely as she passed. It was a long white beard, and China couldn't help noticing that it had bits of toast stuck in it.

"I'm sorry it's such a mess," said Mr Jupiter. He was talking about the house, not the beard. "Sit down, sit down! And tell me about yourself!"

China couldn't see any chairs, only piles of junk. Mr Jupiter was even more untidy than she was! She sat down on an old radio. Mr Jupiter sat down on an old wooden crate. He smiled at China, and stroked his beard.

"Tell me about your family," he said.

"My dad lost his job," said China. "At first he was really depressed but now he's getting into cooking."

"Cooking!" cried Mr Jupiter. "I'm absolutely hopeless! I can't even boil an egg!"

"My mum's starting up a cybercafe," said China. "For the internet, you know?"

"Indeed I do!" cried Mr Jupiter. "Fascinating, fascinating! I like that kind of thing. Have you got any brothers or sisters?"

"I've got a big sister called Rose. We fight all the time."

"Oh no! Don't tell me! More trouble! Everywhere I look is fighting and violence!" Mr Jupiter's fingers started to shake, and he tied the ends of his beard in knots.

"We don't really fight," China reassured him. "Only sort of yell at each other. She's a lot of fun sometimes. But I really hate her boyfriend!"

"Why is that?" asked Mr Jupiter, his head cocked on one side like a bird's.

"I don't know, really," China said. "It's just a feeling I've got. Nick's always cracking jokes, and he's ever so polite with Mum and Dad, but I just don't trust him."

"Follow your instincts, my girl," said Mr Jupiter, shaking his head sadly. "There are people in the world, unfortunately…"

But here he broke off, and looked down at the floor. Along the carpet, right by Staff's nose, there was a trickle of soapy water.

"My!" cried Mr Jupiter. "I was washing the sides when you rang the doorbell. The water must've overflowed!"

They splashed through the hall, and into the kitchen. Water was pouring down – the floor was a lake, and there was a half-eaten biscuit floating across the room, like a little raft.

"Oh dear, oh dear, oh dear!" said Mr Jupiter, turning off the water. "What a mess! I am completely hopeless!"

"I'll help," said China. "That's what I came for, after all! Have you got a sponge or something?"

Soon China was mopping up the mess, while Mr Jupiter watched, twiddling his fingers. China noticed there were little drops of water in his beard. He looked terribly sad.

"There!" she beamed. "That's the worst of it gone. If you keep the window open, it'll soon dry off."

"If only that were true!" sighed Mr Jupiter, sitting down and dropping his head into his hands. "If only—"

"What do you mean?" asked China.

"I can't explain. It's too complicated. But when stupid old Mr Jupiter floods his whole kitchen, other people suffer in the end, my dear."

"It's all right," said China. "I didn't mind a bit."

"You're a good girl, China," said Mr Jupiter, and he almost smiled.

"Let's forget it now. It's all over," said China.

"That's just where you're wrong, my dear," murmured Mr Jupiter. "That's just where you're wrong. It isn't all over. It's only just beginning."

As China walked home, ten minutes later, she couldn't get Mr Jupiter's face out of her mind. He had such frightened eyes! And what did he mean by, "It's only just beginning"? What was beginning?

At her side, Staff bounded along, enjoying his walk, but China felt strangely cold inside. She looked up at the sky. Black clouds were racing in from the west.

"Come on, Staff," she said. "We'll run the rest of the way home."

# 4

The black clouds turned into rain. It poured. The streets were like rivers – old cigarette packets swirled away down the drains, cats lurked on window ledges, hunched up and miserable-looking. But over at the Stadium, it was football as usual. The waves of cheering rose as the waves of rain fell. They met and mingled in a stream of excitement that drifted over the nearby park.

China and Staff were running round the park, in training for another silver cup. China heard the distant cheers and imagined they were cheering her as she swept through the final tape for an Olympic Gold. She wouldn't have been quite so happy if she'd known that one of the voices cheering in that football crowd was Nick's. Yes, smooth-talking, wisecracking Nick, her sister's boyfriend, and China's pet hate.

He stood halfway up the Eastern terrace, watching the ball with half-shut eyes, hands in his pockets. Beside him stood a person of gorilla-like charm. His eyes were too small, his nose was like a squashed turnip, his teeth were brown stumps, and his chin was spotty. Apart from that, he looked just great. His name was Div. It must've been short for something, but even Div had forgotten what.

"Good game," said Div. "Pity Rose couldn't come."

"Ah well," said Nick, stubbing out his cigarette, "her dad's very anti, you know."

"What – anti you?"

"No, no, Div. Anti-football."

"Does he approve of you, then?"

"Oh yeah," smiled Nick, picking his teeth with a split matchstick. "I'm the boy wonder. Friend of the family."

"What, you? You're the perfect boyfriend, are you?" Div's grin was not really very pleasant. Nick's was worse.

"You bet. I'll have old Mrs Lee darning my socks before Christmas."

Div spat his gum out on to the floor. It gleamed

and steamed for a moment and then slowly went hard in the chilly air. This was the kind of contribution you could expect from Div. He didn't really do a great deal for the environment.

"How's Mrs Lee's cybercafe coming along?"

"Just fine, Div. It opens next week."

"Oh great! We could go along there and have a look, couldn't we?"

"We could do better than that, Div," said Nick out of the corner of his mouth.

"How do you mean?"

"Well," Nick went on, suddenly turning and looking Div straight in the eye, "if you got hold of your friend's van, we could nip along there one dark night, and…work a magic trick."

"Eh?"

"A disappearing act, Div."

"What?"

"Make old Mrs Lee's shiny new PCs disappear, get it?"

"You mean…" Div's mouth hung open, and some rain fell in – unluckily for the rain.

"You mean…you'd steal from your own girlfriend's family?"

"Why not? The stuff's all insured. They'll get the value back. And we'd have a few thousands stashed away under our beds."

"A few thousands?" Div's eyes gleamed. They went quite green with greed.

"Sure. You could have a diamond earring."

"Are you serious, Nick?"

"I certainly am."

"But how—?"

"Leave it to me. Don't bother your ugly little head with the details, Div." Nick looked very pleased with himself. "Relax. Enjoy the football. Uncle Nick will fix it up. Remember – I'm a friend of the family."

Half a mile away, China was still running around the park. She was getting pretty fit by now, which was just as well. She was going to need all the strength she could get in the not-too-distant future.

# 5

When she got through the bandstand, China recognised a slim ginger-haired figure under a big black umbrella. It was a skinny boy with glasses.

"Hey, Zak!" she gasped, skidding to a halt, "where are you going?"

"My mum told me to buy some tins of beans in case there's a flood."

"A flood?"

"You know – if it goes on raining, we might be marooned in our house." Zak's eyes grew huge and scared behind his glasses.

"You know, China, water might come pouring in through the front door, and through the windows...we might have to climb up on to the roof...and be rescued by a boat...we might drown!"

Zak wore a badge with a flashing light. It said

*Don't Panic*. But Zak usually panicked just the same.

"If it never stops raining," he went on, "we'll probably all have to go off and live on another planet. Or in another solar system, most like, because—"

"Oh don't start all that space travel business now," said China, "I've got to tell you about Mr Jupiter."

"Who?"

"Mr Jupiter. The old man I visited for my school project. He's really, really strange and really, really nice."

"Really?"

"Yes, really-really! His house is an incredible mess. There's lots of old books and newspapers lying about, and bits of machinery. He's a sort of inventor, I think. But he's ever so absent-minded. Yesterday, he forgot to turn off the water and it went all over the floor, right down his hall and everything."

Zak looked worried. "That could be dangerous with, you know – electricity and things."

"Oh, it was all right in the end," said China. "I helped him clear it all up. I'm going back today."

"Wasn't it boring, then?"

"Boring? No, Mr Jupiter is amazing. He's very, very shy, though. And I think he was afraid of me when he opened the door."

"Maybe he was scared of Staff?"

"Yes – maybe. He's got a long white beard, Zak – he looks just like Father Christmas. Except he's thin, and sort of in a mess."

"It must be awful, being old," sighed Zak, starting across to where a couple of feeble old twenty-year-olds were feeding the birds.

"Yes. But at least I can help him. Do you want to come and see him, too, Zak?"

"I can't today," said Zak. "My mum wants me to stay home in case there's a flood. Honestly! I think she's crazy."

"So's my mum," said China. "She's in a real state. Her cybercafe opens next week."

"Fantastic!" said Zak. "Can I come round and have a go?"

"You'll have to ask her," called China, breaking into a run again. "Come on, Staff – I'll race you home."

"See you, China!" Zak went off, still holding his

umbrella up, although the rain had stopped ages ago.

China splashed her way home through the puddles. Her hair was wet, her track suit steamed, and her shoes were disgustingly squelchy. In fact, she seemed to be fated to get soaked, these days. First, at Mr Jupiter's yesterday, and now this incredible rainstorm...

China wondered about Mr Jupiter. What was he doing, right now? She hoped it wasn't anything too dangerous. She hoped he bought his bread ready-sliced. Because she had a feeling he needed a lot of looking after.

# 6

"Hello again, Mr Jupiter! I've come to look after
you again."

"Hello, China," said Mr Jupiter nervously. There
were crumbs of cheese in his beard, this time. "I'm
so glad to see you. Come in, come in..." He
slammed the door behind them, and a picture fell
off the wall and smashed.

"Oh no!" cried Mr Jupiter. "Watch out for that
broken glass."

"I'll sweep it up for you," China offered. "Where's
your dustpan and brush?"

"Where...ah, er...where indeed. Never mind
that for a moment, China. Have I shown you my
workshop, yet?"

"Your workshop? No."

"Come through here, then," said Mr Jupiter,

pushing his way through a dark doorway. He fumbled for the light switch, and all at once the room was lit up by the glare from a naked bulb. China gasped. She had never seen such a mess. There were piles and piles of machinery everywhere. Some of it was really dusty. There were valves, and switches, and great spaghetti-like swathes of wire discs and dials and screens. Right in the middle of the room, on a small table, was something that looked a bit like an old-fashioned radio.

"What's this?" asked China.

"Ah, this! My own invention. It's called a Cosmotronic Unit."

"Is it like a computer?"

"That's the idea. It has a long-distance scanner, and – oh, all sorts of tricks."

"Can I have a go on it, please? Oh please, Mr Jupiter!" Mr Jupiter looked doubtful, and stroked his beard. He found a bit of cheese in it, peered closely at the cheese, smelt it, and then tossed it away over his shoulder.

"What were you saying, my dear?"

"Your Cosmotronic Unit – may I have a go on it, please?"

"Ah, well…why not?" Mr Jupiter switched it on. A couple of red lights and a cheerful hum showed it was working.

"What would you like to do with it, my dear?"

"Well – what can it do?"

"Let me see…would you like to hear what's going on in your own home?"

"My own home! Can it do that?"

"I think so…" said Mr Jupiter. "Let me see…" He fiddled with the knobs and dials, and tuned it in just like the radio. At first there was a vague crackle, but then China heard the sound of her dad in the kitchen. She knew it was her dad because he was singing "Some Enchanted Evening".

"That's my dad!" she yelled. "Hello, Dad!"

"He can't hear you," explained Mr Jupiter. "But we can hear him, you see." Just then there was a bark, and China's dad stopped clattering the dishes.

"Staff!" he cried. "You bad dog! That's supposed to be for our dinner! Leave it alone! Let go! Let go!"

"Staff must have stolen a bit of meat!" said China, laughing. There was the sound of a scuffle, and China's dad cursed a bit.

"Look at that!" he complained. "You've ruined

my piece of beef! I was going to make Beef Stroganoff with that! Dog's teeth marks all over it! Although, I suppose if I washed it and cut it up, they'd never know, would they?" There came the sound of running water.

"Oh, no!" cried China. "He's washing it! How gross!"

"Seems OK," said China's dad. "Oh well. What they don't know, won't hurt them. Where's that onion..."

Just then there was a kind of whirr, and the Cosmotronic Unit's lights went off.

"Dear, oh dear," muttered Mr Jupiter. "Lost the power again! What's wrong this time?"

"Never mind, Mr Jupiter," said China. "It was great. Just wait till I get home and tell Dad I've been listening to him!"

"Oh, China!" Mr Jupiter looked horrified. His beard practically stood on end. "You mustn't tell him! My dear, I must insist – this is an absolute secret."

"A secret?" asked China, puzzled.

"A deadly secret. You mustn't tell anyone, my dear – promise."

"You mean – it's against the law?" asked China.

"No, no – nothing like that. It's just that I only showed you because I thought I could trust you."

"You can, Mr Jupiter, you can! I won't tell anyone, I promise. Not even Dad."

"Good girl," said Mr Jupiter, looking relieved. "Run along home now. We can have a go with some more machines tomorrow."

As China ran home across the park, she wondered why on Earth Mr Jupiter was making such a fuss. It was all a bit odd, really.

# 7

China's dad had really gone to town with the Beef Stroganoff. Even Rose couldn't resist the smell.

"It's delicious, John!" Mum was thrilled.

"Yes, Dad, fantastic! There's only one thing." China's eyes twinkled. "It tasted a bit, well…doggy."

"Doggy?" gasped Dad, looking amazed and ever so slightly guilty. "Doggy?"

Staff leapt out of his basket and bounded up to the table. "Not you, Staff!" said Dad, hiding his confusion.

"Don't talk nonsense, China," said her mum. "She was always fussy, John. Take no notice."

All the same, Dad gave China a very strange look as they cleared the dishes. China kept a straight face, but inside she was giggling like mad. Mr Jupiter was really great! Just think of the tricks she could play on all her friends! And she absolutely must take Zak along there. It was all too amazing – she simply had to share it.

"Some enchanted evening…" sang Dad as he wiped the table.

"You may see a stranger…" crooned China through the soapsuds.

"What's this?" said a voice in her ear. "I didn't know you could do animal impressions, China."

China whirled round. There stood Nick, grinning his most unpleasant grin. Suddenly, China didn't feel like singing. She turned her back on him and said nothing. It wasn't an enchanted evening, any more.

"How's the business, Mrs Lee?" asked Nick.

"Oh, not bad," sighed China's mum, "but we'll never be ready to open by next week."

"How are you fixed for locks and stuff?" asked Nick. "Got a burglar alarm?"

"My brother said he'd deal with that – but I don't think he's got around to it yet."

"Well, I was just thinking…since I'm an electrician and all, why don't I install one for you? I could get you one cheap, from my boss."

"Why, Nick, how marvellous," said China's mum. China felt sick. The nicer Nick was, the sicker she felt.

"It's no trouble, Mrs Lee," he went on. "You can't be too careful. There's a lot of bad guys around – believe me." And he smiled his most convincing smile.

Nick was as good as his word – or as bad, depending on how you look at it. He got a burglar alarm for Mrs Lee and he fixed it. He fixed it in more ways than one. But Mrs Lee was all gratitude – and not just to his face. She even said how marvellous he was behind his back! It made China grind her teeth with rage.

"And he's always so polite and charming," Mrs Lee was saying next morning at breakfast.

"He's always rude and obnoxious to me!" snapped China.

"Don't be silly," said Rose, "he's only teasing."

"It doesn't feel like teasing. When he pulls my hair, it really hurts. He's a bully!"

"Goodness, China, what a fuss about nothing!" said her mum. "Nick is an extremely nice boy. He's always so considerate and helpful."

"Oh yes – to you! He's always sucking up to you, and sidling around you, trying to get on the right side of you. He's like a slimy, horrible snake."

"Oh shut up, China!' said Rose, and she hit her over the head with *Your Forty Favourite Screen Stars* (it wasn't a heavy magazine, luckily, but it still hurt).

"Why should I shut up?" snapped China, and she grabbed *Your Forty Favourite Screen Stars* and tore a couple of pages out.

"China! China! You beast!" Rose grabbed China by the hair. China grabbed Rose's hair, too, although it was all sticky with gel and felt revolting.

"Stop it! Stop it!" cried Mum.

Staff leapt from his basket and bounced around barking. He thought they were having fun and wanted to have a bit, too. Then Dad ran in, his face covered with shaving foam.

"You girls, cut it out, or else!"

It was suddenly still. Little bits of shaving foam flew off his face when he yelled, and one landed on Staff's nose. "Your mother's worn out and I'm sick to death of looking for work and all you two

37

can do is tear each other limb from limb."

China stood very still and stared at the carpet. Little bits of foam kept landing on it.

"What help do we get from you two? What support? Forget it! All we get is trouble. I wonder why I ever had kids sometimes!" And he stalked back to the bathroom, looking like an angry clown. China saw the two pages she'd torn out of *Your Forty Favourite Screen Stars*, and she felt really disgusted with herself. It was an old movie magazine of her mum's and Rose was always browsing through it. China felt dreadful. She hated damaging Rose's things. And its having been Mum's, once, just made it all worse. But sometimes she just couldn't help herself.

"I'm going to see Mr Jupiter," she growled, and fled. Somehow, when she felt this way, Mr Jupiter was her only hope.

# 8

Zak's mum thought it was safe for him to go out, as it hadn't rained for several hours. So China whisked him away to Mr Jupiter's. She couldn't wait for him to see the Cosmotronic Unit. Maybe they could listen to Zak's mum talking to the cat. Or maybe one of the teachers at school. Or maybe…

"Here we are," said China, and rang Mr Jupiter's jangly old doorbell.

"Hi, Mr Jupiter!" she said as he peeped round the door at them. "This is my friend, Zak Williams. He's completely harmless. I mean, you can really trust him. I wanted him to meet you because you're so amazing and I always have such a great time when I come here."

Mr Jupiter blushed. Even his beard went slightly pink.

"My goodness, China," he said. "I don't deserve such praise. Come in, come in. What was your name? Jack?"

"Zak," said Zak, and his eyes got bigger and bigger as he stepped into the dark chaos where Mr Jupiter lived.

"Can we see your machines, Mr Jupiter, please!" begged China. Mr Jupiter looked doubtful, stroked his beard, found a prawn in it, and tossed it into a broken watering can.

"Zak," he said, "will you solemnly swear not to tell anyone what you're about to see? And I mean it – solemnly swear."

Zak licked his lips and put on his most solemn face. "I swear by the sacred name of Manchester United," he intoned, "I will never tell anybody."

"Not like that, Zak, you idiot," giggled China.

"No, it's all right," said Mr Jupiter. "That'll do just fine. Come along then." And he led the way to the workshop.

When Zak saw the mountains of machinery in there, he swore again – softly, under his breath, and not solemnly at all.

"Can we have a go on the Cosmotronic

Unit, please?" asked China.

"I'm afraid not," said Mr Jupiter. "I took it to bits last night…and I used the interface to build this new machine – it's called Futurefeel." He switched it on, and several green lights started winking.

"It's brilliant!" breathed Zak. "What does it do?"

"It tells you what sort of mood you're going to be in, on any future occasion…I think," said Mr Jupiter. "Sometimes my machines don't turn out quite the way I'd intended."

"Hey!" said Zak, "Could your machine take us forward hundreds of years? Space travel and all that?"

"Oh, no!" groaned China, "that's boring! Zak is space mad, Mr Jupiter, but I hate all that stuff. I'd rather know what's going to happen to me."

"Take care, children," warned Mr Jupiter, with the hint of a glint in his eye. "Maybe it's better not to know what's in store. Maybe in twenty years' time you'll be married – to each other!"

"Ugh – no!" chorused the happy couple. "Gross!"

"WE don't want to know that far ahead," said China. "Just – oh, what's going to happen tonight."

"I know that already," said Zak. "Dinner

41

round your house and then watch TV."

"Oh, go on, Mr Jupiter," said China. "Please."

"Oh, all right," sighed Mr Jupiter, and he twiddled the knobs on his Futurefeel machine. There were some strange electric growls and hums, and the dials whizzled, and then, all of a sudden, a message flashed up on the screen. DANGER, it said. EXTREME DANGER FEAR AND TERROR. China felt a cold thrill of fear go zipping up her back.

"What, us?" she gasped. "Tonight?"

"I expect there's a horror film on TV," said Zak, but his voice was shaking a bit.

"Dear me, dear me." Mr Jupiter was very flustered. "That can't be right. I must have made an error. Programmed it wrong. Let me see…" And he typed their names on the keyboard: *China Lee and Zak Williams*, and the date, and the time – 8:00pm. Once again, the message flashed up, DANGER EXTREME DANGER FEAR AND TERROR. Mr Jupiter switched the machine off. He was very pale. Even his beard was whiter than usual.

"There's definitely a fault," he mumbled. "I'll have to redesign it. Don't worry."

"But what sort of danger?" whispered Zak.

"It was a mistake, Zak." Mr Jupiter smiled as hard as he could but the smile still didn't look right. "Don't worry. Forget it. Now run along home." He shooed them to the door as if he wanted to get rid of them, and as he opened it, China saw that his hand was shaking.

"Off you go, then," he said. "Run along home. And TAKE CARE!" His words echoed strangely in the empty street, and a Coke can rolled along the road, blown by the wind. China's heart gave a frightened quiver.

"Come on, Zak," she said in a wobbly voice. "I'll race you."

# 9

By eight o'clock, China and Zak were feeling pretty good after all. They had devoured China's dad's Pizza Margherita in seconds.

"Oh dear," said Dad, sighing. "I wish I'd taken a photograph of it. It was a work of art. And where is it now? Gone. You need a heart of stone to be one of the world's great chefs."

China and Zak were sitting on the sofa waiting for an old cop movie to start. And hoping there would be a good car chase. Neither of them mentioned the fact that, so far this evening, there had been no sign of any danger, let alone EXTREME DANGER FEAR AND TERROR. In fact, things looked pretty nice right now.

Their only problem was Rose. It was not one of her best evenings. Earlier in the day, she'd soaked for hours in a bubble-bath. Rose had also washed her hair, sat for half an hour with a mudpack on her face and painted her finger and toenails frosted green. And then Nick had rung to wriggle out of their date.

"He's got someone else," she sighed, staring tragically at the sofa cushions.

"Don't raise my hopes," said China, although she felt a bit mean. Rose looked really down. In fact, she was lying on the floor, and you can't get more down than that. China hoped she wouldn't realise there was a weepy film romance on one of the other channels. But it was OK. After a while Rose ambled of to refreeze her nails, and China and Zak settle down to watch the film.

They were only just into the credits when the picture disappeared. Mr Lee tried everything, from a delicate fiddling with the knobs to a hearty thump, but the stupid thing just wouldn't revive.

"Ladies and gentlemen," he announced, "our TV is dead. May I suggest an alternative pleasure this evening – homework?"

"Great joke," said China crossly. "We're in the middle of the holidays. Can we go round and watch it at Zak's house, Dad?"

"OK, OK," sighed Dad. "Far be it from me to ruin our evening."

"Take Staff!" called Mum from the kitchen. "And just check everything's OK as you go past the shop."

It was nearly dark as they raced down Mile Street. There was a bit of traffic about, but no people.

"I expect they're all watching telly," panted China. "Lucky beasts!" They dived down an alley at the side of Surfshack.com, but then they skidded to a halt.

"Hey!" hissed China. "There's a van parked in our yard!" They ducked behind some dustbins and boxes of rubbish, just as a figure wearing a balaclava emerged from the back of the building, carrying a huge box. It was one of Mrs Lee's computers. He loaded it into the van. There seemed to be someone else inside the van.

"Here's the last one!" said the figure. "Is it all nice and secure?"

"You bet," said a voice from inside the van. "And it's as hot as hell in here, with this balaclava on."

"Stop moaning!" said the other. "Put this one in and let's get out of here."

46

China felt sick. Zak was shaking so hard, she could hear his teeth chattering. But Staff was a real hero. He knew the burglars were up to no good. He knew China was scared. He bridled. He showed his teeth. He growled – and all of a sudden, he tore himself free of China's grip and lunged at the van, with a deep snarl breaking into the most furious barking.

"Get off, goddamit!" shouted the man, and leap into the driving seat, slamming the door. The engine leapt into life, the headlamps dazzled China and Zak, the gears crashed, and the van stormed past, knocking the boxes over and blasting China and Zak with carbon monoxide. It swept off down Mile Street, with Staff chasing its tail.

"Come back, Staff!" cried China. "Oh, Zak! He'll get killed!" Zak was trying to brush the bits of rubbish off his jacket.

"Staff! Staff!" screamed China. But all she could hear was Staff's bark, getting fainter and fainter in the distance.

"Oh, no!" she cried. "Please, please God, don't let Staff get hurt." And she burst into tears.

There was no question now about the feelings that flooded into her heart – yes, they were DANGER EXTREME DANGER FEAR AND TERROR.

# 10

Next morning, there was still no sign of Staff. If Staff had been safe at home, China could almost have enjoyed all the excitement of the burglary – giving statements to the police, going through it all again and again, and trying to remember any little detail that might help catch the crooks. But she hadn't even noticed the colour of the van. She was really angry with herself.

She was also in a state about Staff. She'd stopped crying, now, but her eyes were all swollen and red.

"Where is he? Where is he?" she said, walking round and round the room, biting her nails. "They must have killed him. They must have, or he'd have come home by now."

"I'm sure they haven't killed him, China," said Rose. Rose was being really kind. Sometimes she even managed to cheer China up for a minute or two. "I'm sure he'll come back soon. Why don't you try and forget about it for a couple of hours and come swimming with me today?" China always wanted to go swimming with Rose, but Rose usually told her to get lost, and went with Nick instead.

"What about Nick?" asked China.

"I'll tell him I want to go with you today," said Rose. "He won't mind. He's got things to do."

Just then, the doorbell rang. China raced to answer it. It could be someone bringing Staff home! Or maybe the police had caught the burglars! China threw the door open – and there stood Nick. China burst into tears.

"China's had a terrible experience," explained Rose, as Nick came in. "She saw two guys stealing all Mum's stuff last night, and Staff chased them and he hasn't come back. Poor China."

Nick looked very serious. For once there was no smile, no teasing. He even went quite pale at the news.

"Hey, China, kid!" he said. "I'm sure Staff's OK. But did you say you saw the guys?"

"I saw one of them," sniffed China, drying

her eyes. "The other was in the van."

"What was he like? Would you recognise him again?"

"China's already been through all that with the police, Nick," said China's mum. "She's had enough of it. Don't go on."

"It's all right, Mum," said China, standing up and putting her jacket on. "I hardly saw anything. He had all dark clothes on and he was wearing a balaclava. I'd never be able to identify him again."

"Too bad," said Nick. "Did you notice anything about the van?"

"Nothing. Not even the colour. It was all over so fast." China zipped up her jacket, and for a split second, looked round to Staff's basket as she always did when she went out for a walk.

"Where are you going, China?" asked her mum.

"I think I'll go and see Mr Jupiter."

"Good idea, sweetheart! He usually manages to cheer you up."

"Tell you what, China," said Nick. "I'll go out and look for Staff. I don't suppose I'll see anything. But I can cruise round the streets in my car. You never know."

51

"Thanks, Nick," said China, in a dull kind of voice. It seemed strange, Nick acting so kind and concerned. Maybe he was a good guy after all – underneath. But China couldn't be bothered to think about that at the moment. All she could think of was the way she'd felt, three years ago, when a dear little bundle of black fur on wobbly legs had tottered across the carpet towards her, and her Dad had said, "Happy Birthday, China! Our present unwrapped himself – here he is!" And the little puppy had licked her face. Ever since then, she and Staff had been together. But she was on her own now. It had never seemed so far across the park.

"Please, please, God," whispered China as she passed the bandstand, "make it so Staff comes back safe and well. If you do, I promise I'll always keep my room tidy and I'll never get mad at Rose again." A cloud of dust blew into her eyes. It didn't seem very encouraging.

China picked up Zak, who was hanging about by the ice-cream van, and they went to Mr Jupiter's. China had a feeling that Mr Jupiter could help her. More than that, she felt he was her only hope.

"Oh, Mr Jupiter!" China burst out, as soon as he

opened the door. "Something terrible's happened! Really, really awful! It was last night – just like your machine predicted!"

"DANGER EXTREME DANGER FEAR AND TERROR!" added Zak.

"Oh, dear me, no!" gasped Mr Jupiter. "I can't bear it. Don't tell me! No, of course I don't mean that – it's just that everything's in such a mess! So out of control! The Planet Earth is in complete chaos. Not to mention this house. I always bite off more than I can chew."

"Pardon?" asked Zak. China's heart sank. It didn't seem as if Mr Jupiter was going to be any help, after all. He seemed to be even more shaken up than they were.

"Take no notice... take not notice," he said. "I'm just flabbergasted, that's all! Tell me about it." So China and Zak told Mr Jupiter about the robbery and the getaway, and Staff disappearing. As he listened, Mr Jupiter seemed to become less and less flabbergasted and more and more angry. He began to stride up and down.

"Really!" he thundered. "How can people be so wicked? I can't believe it! If ever I catch sight of

these burglars they'll be sorry they were ever born!"
His eyes sort of flashed, and China thought she
heard his beard crackle – but perhaps it was only the
toast crumbs. She'd never seen Mr Jupiter get
angry before.

"The worst thing is," she went on, "that my dog's
gone! I'm sure they've killed him! Oh, it's awful! If
anything's happened to Staff, I think I'll die!"

"Now now, China, don't despair," said Mr Jupiter.
"You never know, I might be able to help."

"Oh, could you, Mr Jupiter? Oh, please, please get
Staff back for me. I knew you'd help."

"Don't count your chickens," warned Mr Jupiter,
"before they're…you know…whatsitted." He
wandered over to a very rickety-looking piece of
machinery – it looked like a dented computer
screen linked up to an old-fashioned wireless set.
On the top were three glass tubes full of purple
liquid that bubbled and smoked.

"This is my Canine-ometer," said Mr Jupiter. "It's
all to do with dogs, you see."

'What can it do?" asked China.

"It can kill fleas within a radius of three miles.
It can throw sticks. And sometimes it can find lost

dogs."

"Oh, Mr Jupiter! Fantastic!"

"Only sometimes, mind you. Don't get over-excited, China. It may not work. If…"

"I know, I know, Mr Jupiter. But at least we'll have tried! Please!"

"Let me see…" said Mr Jupiter, fiddling with the machine. "Staffordshire Bull Terrier…name Staff…owner…China Lee…now, locate, and indicate position." He punched the commands into the keyboard. The screen flickered and hesitated, and suddenly there, crystal clear, was Staff! He was barking and jumping up at a doorway.

"It's Staff!" screeched China. "Where is he? Where is it?"

"Calm down, China," complained Mr Jupiter. "You'll give me one of my headaches, and then, well…things can get really catastrophic, my dear."

"Sorry," whispered China, "but what about Staff?"

"I'll try and get a bigger picture," said Mr Jupiter. "That'll give us some idea of where he is."

Suddenly the picture on the screen zoomed away backwards, to reveal—

"The fried chicken place!" yelled Zak.

"That's right! It really, really is! I'll go and get him, Mr Jupiter! Thanks very much! Your machine is brilliant!"

"Be careful, China!" warned Mr Jupiter. "And good luck!"

China and Zak flew down the street.

"He's always sniffing round the fried chicken place," said China. "Let's hope he's still there!"

Yes. There he was – and when he saw China, he gave a great leap and flung his front paws right round her shoulders.

"Oh, Staff, Staff!" she yelled. "It's really you! It's really, really you! How fantastic! Let's go home and tell Mum! Come on!"

As they ran home, China remembered a promise.

Thanks a million, God! she thought. For helping us – for making Mr Jupiter find—

But then, all of a sudden, a most peculiar thought came into her head. Such a very peculiar idea, that she suddenly stopped running and the traffic and the street and the whole world seemed to change into slow motion, and silence. It was the strangest idea China had ever had. So strange, it made her go hot and cold all over, as if she had dipped a toe into another dimension.

# 11

"What is it, China?" asked Zak. China had such a strange look in her face. "What's the matter? Do you feel bad?"

"No…no, Zak. I've just had such a weird idea."

"What?" Zak felt himself go pale. It was a creepy feeling, somehow. Terrible and yet quite exciting.

"I think there's something funny about Mr Jupiter."

"You mean, he's off his head?"

"No, no. I mean, he's…well, not a normal human being."

Zak gasped with longing.

"You mean he's an alien? From Outer Space?"

"Not exactly. Not really an alien. More, you know…supernatural, sort of thing."

"What, like a ghost?"

"No, Zak – don't be stupid! I mean, like a god or something."

"A god?" Zak burst out laughing. "Honestly, China! A god? I mean, gods are supposed to be all powerful and things. I mean, Mr Jupiter is just a cranky old man."

"But think what he can do with those machines."

"You don't have to be a god to invent brilliant machines."

"But he's always worried about the state of the world!"

"So's my mum, but she's not a goddess."

"No, but Mr Jupiter, well, he kind of acts as if he's you know – responsible. He gets all upset when you tell him bad news."

"Who doesn't?"

"And what he said just now! He said if he gets one of his headaches, things can get really catastrophic."

"My mum gets catastrophic headaches, too. One time she threw a whole salad at my dad's head."

"Be serious, Zak! This could be why Mr Jupiter's so secretive – why he doesn't want us to tell anyone about him."

"Or it could be he's just a little bit crazy."

China felt disappointed that Zak was so unconvinced. The more she thought about it, the more she was absolutely sure she was right. But Zak remained sceptical.

"If there was a god, wouldn't he be living in heaven? Why would he want to live in Lordship Road of all places? It's a really crummy street."

"Well, gods do things like that. They like to be incognito."

"But surely – if he was a god – he'd live in a big house by a beach somewhere with lots of servants and guard dogs and a swimming pool."

"I'm talking about a god, Zak!" yelled China. "Not a film star. Honestly! You're so stupid sometimes."

"But if he was a god," Zak went on, "why would his house be in such a mess? He would have angels to clear it up for him."

"Zak Williams," said China. "You're an idiot!"

"Why do people have to be idiots if they just don't agree with you?" asked Zak.

China sighed. "OK, OK. Forget I said anything. Let's take Staff home."

By the time they got home, China had cheered up again. Staff was overjoyed to see the rest of the family. Rose even let him lick her face, though she'd only just finished putting on her make-up.

"I wonder how far Staff followed the van?" said China's mum.

"Not very far," said Dad. "Dogs can't compete with the engine power of a big truck like that."

"If only Staff could talk," said China. "Maybe he could tell us something. He could be a very important witness."

Just then, the doorbell rang. Rose answered it and Nick walked in.

"Hey!" he said. "Staff's back! That's terrific!"

But Staff acted very strangely. He paused for a moment, stared at Nick, and then all of a sudden he flew at him, barking furiously and snapping at his legs.

"Come back, Staff! Stop it!" yelled China, and dragged him by the collar into the nearest bedroom. She pushed him in and slammed the door shut.

"I'm really really sorry, Nick," she said. "He's probably all upset after his adventure, you know."

"Sure," said Nick, brushing dog hairs off his

sleeve. "It's OK. I know what it was. I've just been round at my uncle's, and I was stroking a cat there."

"Ah, yes!" said Rose. "That must be it. Staff hates cats."

"So does our dog," said Zak.

"Anyway, I'd better not hang around here getting up Staff's nose, as it were," said Nick. "Are you ready to go, Rose?" Rose was. They were all set for the club, where Nick had promised to meet Div, and Div's girlfriend. If Div could manage to find one by then.

"Bye, China," said Nick. "I'm glad you got your doggie back."

"Such a nice boy," said Mrs Lee as the door closed behind them. "He was out looking for Staff for hours this morning, China."

"Oh…yes," murmured China, but her mind wasn't on the conversation. After Zak had gone home, China let Staff out of the bedroom and stroked his firm black back. She stared into his kind brown eyes.

"Staff," she whispered, "why did you fly at Nick just now? Why, Staff?"

But Staff refused to comment.

# 12

Rose was in the loos in the club, staring into the mirror. She wasn't enjoying herself as much as she'd hoped. For a start, they were landed with Nick's friend, Div. He was by himself, and Rose wasn't surprised. No self-respecting girl would have anything to do with a guy that gross. She was surprised that Nick was a friend of his. But then, everyone liked Nick. At least if Div hadn't brought a girlfriend, that meant there was one less girl making eyes at Nick through the flashing lights.

Mind you, Nick wasn't in all that good a mood, either. He seemed strangely uneasy tonight – absent, even, as if his thoughts were elsewhere. Rose began to panic. Had he fallen for another girl? Was he wondering how to break it to her? Feverishly, she rolled another layer of lipstick on. But even that didn't make her look irresistible.

Out in the club itself, Nick and Div were standing by a wall. Nick wasn't thinking about Rose's looks, though. He wasn't thinking about Rose at all. Or any other girl, for that matter.

"Listen," he said, right in Div's ear, because of the noise, "calm down. If your nerves can't take it, at least keep your mouth shut. We're home and dry. We'll never get caught."

"Oh, yeah," muttered Div. "I just want my cut. Come on, Nick. I'm broke. I can't even afford a beer."

"All in good time. All the stuff is safely stashed away. Tomorrow, I'm going to see a dealer who'll take it off our hands."

"So I'll get my money tomorrow?"

"Tomorrow or the next day."

"Great! I'm going to get myself a new bike. A Harley Davidson vintage—"

"There's just one thing that bothers me," Nick went on.

"What's that?"

"Those kids. They say they didn't see anything, but you never know. The goddamned dog nearly took a chunk out of my leg tonight. And that China is a clever little kid. Too clever by half."

"You mean…?"

"If China and that kid, Zak, get suspicious…well, I'll have to think of something."

"What?"

"Something to shut 'em up."

"What do you mean?"

"Fit 'em with silencers, you know… permanently."

"You don't mean—"

"I don't know what I do mean, to tell you the truth."

"You wouldn't do anything rash, would you, Nick?"

"I don't know what I might not do, if I was pushed." Nick prepared one of his most convincing smile. He could see Rose making her way towards them through the crowd.

"C'mon, Rose!" He flung his arm round her. "Let's let our hair down. We've got a lot to celebrate."

"Have we?" asked Rose. "What?"

"Your sister's got her dog back, nobody got hurt,

your mum will get the insurance money, no harm done, eh?"

Rose was glad that Nick seemed to have shaken off his thoughtful mood.

"C'mon, babe, get on down." A hip-hop number blasted across the floor. Nick tossed Div a couple of bank notes.

"Hey, Div!" he grinned. "Drown your sorrows. Buy yourself a beer. Or find a beautiful girl and buy her a lemonade!" And he dashed off laughing into the flashing lights.

# 13

Next day, China barely touched her breakfast. Rose was still dozy from her late night, and Mum was on the phone to the insurance company. Dad was studying fish recipes from Indonesia. So no one noticed that China didn't eat much. She put an apple in her pocket and ran to the door, calling Staff.

"I'm going to see Mr Jupiter with Zak, OK?" And she was gone.

"She seems to be round at this Mr Jupiter's house all the time, these days," said her mum, putting some papers in her briefcase. "I hope she's not making a nuisance of herself."

"Do we have any green ginger?" asked Dad.

Meanwhile, China ran into the park and met Zak by the bandstand.

"Zak!" she hissed. "I've got something very, very important and serious to tell you."

"Not again!" said Zak. "Is it more about Mr Jupiter being a god?"

"No, it's Nick."

"What about him? Is he a god, too?"

"Don't be stupid! You know the way Staff flew at Nick last night and nearly took a bite out of him?"

"Because of that cat smell?"

"I don't believe that! I think Nick was one of the burglars and Staff recognised him by his smell."

"But Nick wouldn't do that," said Zak. "Not rob your mum's business. I mean, he even fixed her burglar alarm for her."

"Precisely! He probably fixed it in a special way so it would be easier for him to break in, later."

"Nobody's going to believe you, China."

"Don't you believe me?"

Zak scratched his head. "I don't know. You haven't got any proof, have you? I mean, it's so, you know. To rob his girlfriend's family and everything."

"I see," said China. "You don't believe me. I know who will, though – Mr Jupiter. I'll go and see him right now and tell him all about it. Are you coming?"

Zak hesitated. He felt he'd let China down, somehow. But then, recently, her ideas had been getting wilder and wilder. Although Zak was crazy about the idea of Outer Space, he was a pretty cautious and conventional sort of boy underneath.

"No, I don't think I can come this time," he said. "I'd better go home. My mum has got one of her cata-whatsit headaches."

So China went to Mr Jupiter's on her own. He was delighted to see her, of course. But he noticed right away that she wasn't her usual bubbly self.

"What's wrong, China?" he asked, sitting her down on an old filing cabinet and giving her a stale biscuit to eat.

"I've been having some really strange ideas," confessed China. "About Rose's boyfriend, Nick."

"What exactly, my dear?"

"I'm sure he's one of the burglars."

"What? The ones who raided your mother's business?"

"Yes. When he came round last night, Staff went berserk and practically ripped him to pieces. Staff's never done that before. You

69

know dogs have a terrific sense of smell?"

Mr Jupiter smiled privately.

"Yes," he said, nodding. "I've always been rather pleased with that idea."

"Well, I'm sure Staff recognised Nick as one of the burglars."

Mr Jupiter stroked his beard, frowning doubtfully.

"But would your sister's boyfriend do such a terrible thing?"

"I don't know," said China. "I need proof. Can you help me, Mr Jupiter? You're my only hope. Please, please – oh please!"

# 14

Mr Jupiter started to fiddle about with one of his machines. It was really rusty and covered with cobwebs.

"This might do the trick," he murmured. "It's called the Yesterday Machine. It reviews the recent past, you know. If we tune it to your sister's boyfriend – what's his name?"

"Nick Malin."

"Right," said Mr Jupiter, punching the information on to a very old keyboard, "I'll try and get some idea of what he was up to yesterday."

On the top of the Yesterday Machine was an ancient gramophone horn and as Mr Jupiter worked, it began to crackle and buzz like the sound of a very old record. Then, unmistakably, China

heard a *thump, thump, thump* sound of clubbing…
and above it, Nick's voice.

*"If China and that kid, Zak, get suspicious…well, I'll
have to think of something."*

*"What?"*

*"Something to shut 'em up."*

*"What do you mean?"*

*"Fit 'em with silencers, you know… permanently."*

The broadcast ended abruptly with a bang and a
whiff of smoke.

"Good heavens," cried Mr Jupiter. "You were
right, China! How disgraceful!"

"You see? You see? It was him!"

"But you must be very careful, my dear – you're in
danger."

"It's all right, Mr Jupiter! I've got proof now, so I
can tell the police."

"Dear me, n-n-no!" stammered Mr Jupiter. "Not
the police, China, please! They make me nervous."
His hands started to shake, and he began tying his
beard in knots. Suddenly, China felt absolutely sure
of everything. She had to say it, she absolutely
had to.

"Mr Jupiter," she began, her heart hammering,

72

"there's something...something unusual about you, isn't there?"

Mr Jupiter jumped slightly.

"Not at all, my dear. I'm just a foolish old man."

"A foolish old man who can rescue lost dogs and see into the past and the future...I don't think you're an ordinary human being, are you, Mr Jupiter?"

Mr Jupiter got up and moved nervously backwards towards the kitchen, treading on nuts and bolts as he went.

"What do you mean, child? What am I, then?"

"I think you're a supernatural," said China. "You know, like a sort of god."

"China! Please!" whispered Mr Jupiter. "Not so loud! Have you got any idea what would happen to me if such an idea got out?"

"What?"

"I'd end up under arrest or worse. They'd think I was raving mad."

"But you're not mad, are you, Mr Jupiter? I am right, aren't I?"

Mr Jupiter appeared to pull himself together. He kicked a few bits of machinery out of his way, took a deep breath, and faced up to China.

"You're entitled to your opinion, China. You can think what you like. But for heaven's sake don't tell anybody. The important thing for you to do now is go straight home and tell your parents that you think Nick is the burglar."

"OK."

"Make sure that they understand that you're in danger. But don't mention me! Please!"

"I promise."

"Because, if you do…" he hesitated, and looked rather wildly around the room, "I might not be here when you come back – do you understand?"

China nodded. Although Nick might be planning all sorts of nasty tricks with her in mind, she had never felt so excited. She knew she was right about Nick, and she knew she was right about Mr Jupiter. So from here on it would be plain sailing, wouldn't it?

# 15

So, China knew for sure that Nick was one of the burglars. All she had to do was tell her parents, and everything would be all right. She was almost bursting with the news as she rushed in.

"Dad! Mum!" she cried. "I've got something really, really important to tell you— oh!" She skidded to a halt. For who was sitting there having a cup of coffee, but Nick. Nick, the ideal date, the friend of the family.

"Hey, China!" he said. "Something really important? What is it?"

China felt herself go very red. She started to stammer.

"I…I just…had a great time with Mr Jupiter."

"How was he today, China?" asked Mum.

"All right," said China. She realised suddenly

that it was a mistake to have mentioned Mr Jupiter. She didn't want to talk about him. Indeed, she must not. Especially to Nick.

"Mr Jupiter?" Nick cocked an eyebrow. "Who's he?"

"He's an old man she goes to visit sometimes," said Mum, as China was drinking a glass of water and seemed unable to answer.

"What's he like?" asked Nick.

"He's OK," muttered China, getting out a book.

"What's the matter with you, China?" asked her mum. "Do you feel all right?"

"I've got a bit of a headache," lied China. Although she might well be getting one soon, if things went on like this.

"Tell us about Mr Jupiter, China," said Nick. But China was silent, biting her nails.

"China says he's got lots of weird machines in his house," said Rose.

"Has he? Like what?"

"Oh, videos and computers and things, only better. Wasn't it, China?"

China nodded dumbly. If only they would talk about something else! The weather, the price of baked beans, anything.

"Where does he live?" asked Nick.

China felt a pang of fear. Somehow she had to protect Mr Jupiter from Nick. But Rose was determined to give Nick all the help she could.

"It's Lordship Road, isn't it, China? That house at the top – the really scruffy one with the yellow paint. Isn't that right, China?"

China nodded again. The room seemed full of terrible danger, and only she could see.

"Does he live on his own?" asked Nick.

"Yes, but China helps him with the housework and stuff, don't you, China?"

"You'll be getting a medal one day, China!" said Nick. Then he started telling Mrs Lee how great her chocolate cake was – and Mrs Lee reminded him that it was Dad who did the cooking around here, nowadays.

"It's an Austrian recipe," explained Dad. "Have a slice, China." But China didn't want one. She felt sick. She got the feeling that Nick had found out all he needed to know about Mr Jupiter.

Even after Rose and Nick went out, China's stomach was churning with nerves. She had to tell her parents about Nick – but how? She sat at the table, but she couldn't eat a thing. The feeling inside her got heavier and heavier. She felt as if she had swallowed a lead football. Her mum and dad exchanged glances. This wasn't like China. She played with her fork. She heaved a great sigh.

"What is it, China?" asked her mum. China took her courage in both hands.

"Mum, Dad," she said in a trembling voice. "I know who one of the burglars was."

"Who?"

"It was Nick."

"Nick?" chorused her parents, and China knew immediately they'd never believe her. Her dad burst out laughing. Her mum rolled her eyes towards heaven.

"Honestly, China! How could you say such a thing? He's been going out with Rose for months. And he's such a nice boy."

"Ask yourself, China," said her dad, "does it make sense? Would he rob his own girlfriend's family?"

"And when Staff went missing, he was out looking for him – for hours."

"That just shows how clever he is," China said.

"What an imagination, eh?" said Dad. "I can't imagine where she gets it from."

"I'm not imagining it, Dad!" cried China. "I'm sure! And I've got proof."

"What proof?"

"I can't tell you."

"Now you're just being ridiculous."

"I'm not, Mum!" said China. "I just can't tell you. I just can't."

Mum felt her brow. "What you need, love, is a nice lie-down. Go to bed now and I'll bring you a cup of cocoa."

China stood up, reluctantly, and faced her parents.

"Aren't you going to do anything, then? About Nick? You've got to tell the police. He's really, really dangerous."

"No more of that, now, love," said China's mum. "We'll talk about it again in the morning."

So China went to bed, sad, defeated, but still defiant. Staff curled up on her bedside rug.

"I know I'm right," she whispered, leaning down and stroking Staff's head. "And I'll never change my mind. But – oh, however shall I persuade them?"

And, though she wasn't in the least bit ill, she had a terrible feeling in the pit of her stomach. A feeling that things were going to get a lot, lot worse.

# 16

China lay awake for hours, tossing and turning and wondering what on earth to do next. She heard Nick's car draw up outside, and Rose jump out. She heard Rose call "Good night!" as she ran up the steps. And she was glad to hear Nick's car roar off down the road. If her mum and dad told Rose what China had said about Nick being one of the burglars, there'd be an almighty row. Rose would certainly scalp her. China ducked her head under the covers and pretended to be asleep.

China might not have known what to do next, but Nick knew exactly what to do. He drove like a demon over to the crumbling old tenement where Div lived – in a tiny room with rain coming in through the roof.

"You ought to get yourself a new place," observed Nick, scraping the mould off the walls with his fingernail. "You know – now you're a man of the world with a bit of real money behind you. Get yourself out of this hole and into somewhere with a bit of class."

Div looked gloomy.

"What money?" he grumbled. "I blew it all on that motorbike."

"Too bad you crashed it." Nick shook his head. "First time out, too. Bad luck, Div. But cheer up. Fancy a drink? I know a club that's still open."

"No," said Div. "I'm broke. Haven't got a bean. "Don't feel like going out anyway. There's nothing to celebrate."

"That's just where you're wrong, Div," said Nick. "So you need more money? That can easily be arranged."

"What do you mean? You got another job planned?"

"Interested?"

"Maybe."

"There's this old guy, see? Called Mr Jupiter. Lives in Lordship Road. Well…" Nick's eyes brightened.

82

"Apparently his place is full of hardware. VCRs, PCs, wide-screen TV's, DVD players, you name it."

"So?"

"So he's a sort of inventor, see? His place must be full of red-hot stuff. Everybody's after it. New ideas, get it?"

"You mean…we raid his place?"

"A nice gentle little visit, Div. And we borrow a few of his inventions, you know…to see what interest we can raise in the industry."

Div's eyes went dull. Nick was using too many long words.

"Selling ideas, see what I mean?" Nick went on. "And think what you could do with an extra couple of thousand, Div. A holiday in Ibiza. Sun, sea, beautiful girls, and as much vodka as you can drink."

"OK," said Div, looking at his mouldy walls. "Just this once. This is the last time, though, Nick."

"Sure," said Nick. "OK then. I'll drop round sometime tomorrow and we'll make plans. The old team is back in action."

He stepped out on to Div's balcony. The moon was very bright above the rooftops. Somewhere in an alley below, a cat yowled. In the far distance, a police car's siren wailed through the night.

"So, watch out, Mr Jupiter," whispered Nick to the listening dark. "We're on our way."

# 17

China lay in bed till late. She hadn't really wanted to go to bed at all, but now she was there, she didn't want to get up. It was a cosy cave, and with the covers over her head she could kid herself that Mr Jupiter was safe in his rickety old house, that her mum and dad believed in her, and that Nick was a really nice guy and not a burglar at all. He'd never robbed her mum and he'd never threatened to fit China with a silencer – permanently. All that was a bad dream. Yes, she was cosy and warm in her cave. And then—

"China! You absolute pig!"

Suddenly, China's bedcovers were ripped back, and Rose was hitting her with a rolled-up copy of her mum's *Good Housekeeping*. It was a really thick magazine, and it hurt like mad.

"Stop it, Rose! Stop it!"

"It's what you need – a good hiding. Dad should have given you one long ago!"

China sprang out of bed, ran to Rose's side of the bedroom and swept all her neatly arranged jars and bottles off the shelf.

"Leave me alone!" she yelled. "Or I'll stamp on your CDs."

"You're completely off your head, China Lee!" screamed Rose. "Mum just told me what you said about Nick. How could you?"

"It's true, Rose!" said China. "I'm sorry, but it's true. I've got proof."

"What proof?"

"I can't tell you. I just absolutely can't."

"You're completely mad, China."

"You're the one who's mad. You're mad to go out with him. And Mum and Dad are mad to let you."

Rose started picking up her bottles and jars. She was strangely silent. Then China noticed that her shoulders were shaking.

"What's the matter, Rose?" she asked.

"Nick has enough problems of his own

without you making things worse for him!"

"What problems?"

"You don't know anything about Nick, China. He's had a really awful life. And all you can do is tell horrible lies about him!"

"What's wrong, then? What's his problem?"

Rose sat down on her bed and blew her nose.

"I hate crying," she said. "It makes my nose shine."

China scampered across and crouched at her feet.

"I'm sorry I said it, Rose," she whispered. "But I can't help what I think. Tell me about Nick."

"I'll just tell you one thing," said Rose. "His mum couldn't keep him when he was a little baby, so she gave him away. And he had some foster parents but they gave him away too. He spent most of the time in a children's home. It was awful – he got beaten up."

China felt sorry for Nick for a split second. What a terrible start to life. How lucky she was to have her own mum and dad – yes, and even Rose.

"I'm glad I've got you to fight with, Rose," she said. "And I'm sorry Nick had a bad time when he was a kid. I won't say any more about it. But just promise me one thing."

"What?"

"Promise not to tell Nick what I said about him," begged China. "Please, please! If you tell him…I don't know what he'll do."

"You are an idiot," said Rose, affectionately.

She hit China once more over the head with *Good Housekeeping* – only gently, this time – and then strolled off downstairs. China was left with a pounding heart. If Rose told Nick, as she was almost bound to do…what then? Would Rose finally be made to realise that China had been right all along? But would it be too late by then? China crawled back into bed and pulled the covers right over her head.

# 18

China stayed in bed for a couple of days, until even her mum began to think that she wasn't ill any more – if she ever had been. Zak came round to visit, once.

"I bought you some grapes," he said, "but I ate them on the way. And I reckon you're right, China, about…you know who."

"Mr Jupiter?"

"No – Nick. I've been thinking about it and I'm sure one of the men in masks had a voice exactly like Nick's."

This finally prompted China to get up. She had to do something about this whole mess. She couldn't just hide. She arranged with Zak to meet the next day at Mr Jupiter's. He would know what to do. Then she had a bath, and made herself a huge cheese and peanut sandwich.

"You must be better," observed her dad. "You've started making a mess again. That's always a sign of life."

Next day, China met Zak at Mr Jupiter's. They rang the jangly bell and waited. But there was no sound of slippers in the hall. They rang again, beginning to feel nervous. Silence. China could hear her heart beating in the stillness.

"There's something wrong," she said, and jumped into the garden. Then she scrambled up over some old oilcans until she could see in at the window.

"Oh, Zak!" she screamed. "I can see him! He's all tied up! Poor Mr Jupiter!"

Zak tried the front door, and it swung open.

"We're coming, Mr Jupiter!" he yelled, and they both burst in. Mr Jupiter was lying in the middle of his workshop, tied up and gagged. China struggled to untie the gag. Her fingers felt paralysed and useless. Mr Jupiter's eyes looked so frightened, she almost burst into tears.

"Two of them, two of them!" he gasped, as the gag came off. "Stole all my machines!"

Zak ran to get him a drink of water, and

China held his hand.

"Got to stop them – got to stop them!" said Mr Jupiter. "Two robbers. Just like yours. Wearing balaclava masks."

"I bet it was the same ones," said China through clenched teeth. "The beasts! Did they hurt you?"

"No, no – not at all, but my dear – they stole the Earth Destruct machine! They've got to be stopped."

"The Earth Destruct machine?" asked Zak. "Is that a video game?"

"It's a lot more serious than a game, my boy," cried Mr Jupiter, wild-eyed. "It could mean the end of the world."

"What?" gasped China.

"You see – I had to have a machine," said Mr Jupiter. "In case things on Earth got too awful – a machine to destroy the lot in a fraction of a second. So I could start again."

"Mr Jupiter!" cried China.

"I would never have used it, China," he went on. "In fact, I'd forgotten I'd got it. But they found it."

"Oh, no!" said Zak. His eyes were enormous. So China was right, after all! He felt a panic coming on.

"I tried to warn them," said Mr Jupiter. "But I was gagged – gagged, you see."

"So, if they try to play with this machine—" began China, a terrible shaking beginning to spread through her.

"That's right, my dear," groaned Mr Jupiter, "they could destroy the Earth. All they have to do is press the Earth Destruct button."

"Oh, Mr Jupiter!"

"And that'll be the end of us all."

# 19

"Chicken chow mein – that's yours," said Div.

"Yeah – chicken chow mein – that's mine," said Nick. They were sitting in Div's grimy room, surrounded by bits of Mr Jupiter's machinery, and little boxes of Chinese food.

"I don't go much for this Chinese food," grumbled Div. "I nearly choked to death on a beansprout once."

"Ah, well," grinned Nick, "better luck next time."

"I don't know why you're looking so pleased with yourself," said Div. "That old man didn't have anything worth taking. It's a load of old junk we got here." And he slurped disgustingly on his bamboo shoots, feeling rather clever for once.

"That's just where you're wrong, Div," answered

Nick. "But then, that's your trouble – no imagination."

"I don't need imagination to see that you'll have a job getting rid of this lot," Div went on. "You'll have to pay the scrap-metal guys to take it off your hands."

Nick leaned back with a clever smile on his face. "Oh, yeah?" he grinned. "Wanna bet?"

"Well," said Div, kicking a control knob that had dropped off, "what use is it?"

"Listen, Div. This stuff might be prototypes for our new video games. If we could get a company interested, we could make a bomb selling the idea – get it?"

Div gawped. He could just about wrap his brain around the concept. So – these bits and pieces might have a value, after all? Div wandered over to a grey metal machine and brushed the dust off it.

"This one's called Earth Destruct," he said. "I've never seen one like this before. I expect it's a version of the latest Tomb Raider Game. Plug it in, Nick, and let's have a go."

"Where's the socket, then?" asked Nick, finishing his chow mein, and wiping his hands on a handkerchief.

Div pointed across the room to where the socket was. Then he found the cable leading to the Earth Destruct machine, and cursed.

"There's no plug."

"Easily put right, Div. I'm an electrician, remember?" Nick whipped out his screwdriver and twiddled the screws out of another plug – the one on Div's stereo. Then, Nick attached the plug to the Earth Destruct machine, in a leisurely way, as if he had all the time in the world.

Twirl, twirl, twirl, went the screwdriver. Meanwhile, the Planet Earth rolled along, all unsuspecting in its scarves of cloud, its brilliant seas gleaming blue-grey, its birds wheeling across the island trees, its animals resting in noonday heat, its monkeys swinging through the steamy forests.

And man, the cleverest of all its animals, making money and cheating his neighbour in every corner of the globe. Twirl, twirl, twirl, went the screwdriver. And now the plug was ready to connect, the electricity poised to flash – for maybe the biggest shock of all time.

# 20

Back at Mr Jupiter's, China was making a cup of tea. It was what her mum always did in moments of crisis. And if the end of the world isn't a crisis, what is? As she waited for the kettle to boil, she looked out of Mr Jupiter's back window. The sun was shining on the brambles and nettles that grew tall in Mr Jupiter's back garden. It seemed such an ordinary day. China could hardly believe that it all might end, at any moment, with a terrifying flash.

Meanwhile, in the workshop, Mr Jupiter and Zak were panicking. Mr Jupiter was scuttling about amidst the few fragments of machinery he had left, trying in vain to make a jamming device.

"To stop them using the Earth Destruct button, you see, Zak," he said.

"But if they do," asked Zak, his face kind of green

and purple with fear, "can you save us, Mr Jupiter? Couldn't you beam us off to another galaxy? And could you save my mum and dad, too? And my sister – I suppose…"

"It's no use," said Mr Jupiter. "I haven't got the necessary spare parts. They've taken everything – everything! Even my soldering iron. Oh dear, oh dear! That it should come to this! It's bad enough that the world should blow itself up on purpose – but by accident – ah, that's too bad, really quite dreadful!"

"Come and have a cup of tea, Mr Jupiter!" called China.

"My dear China! A capital idea! If we have to face the end of the world, let's do it in style, eh? Let's have tea and toast!"

"Toast! Great!" said Zak. If the world was going to end in a few minutes, he certainly wanted to pack in as much eating as possible before then.

"I think I have some bits of old bread somewhere," murmured Mr Jupiter, peering doubtfully under a pile of coiled wire. "Ah – here it is!"

The bread didn't look terribly appetising. It was slightly grimy and a bit ragged.

"Never mind," said Mr Jupiter. "You won't notice that once it's toasted. Now, where's the toaster? It always used to be over here on the floor – between the goldfish bowl and my football boots."

China looked around.

"Maybe they've stolen the toaster, too," she suggested. Then she found it – in Mr Jupiter's shopping basket. She took it out, dusted it down, and plugged it in.

"Right!" said Mr Jupiter, flourishing two stale slices, "here we go, then!"

Staff wagged his tail. He was looking forward to a nice crispy crust to chew.

But somehow, Mr Jupiter's beard got caught in the toaster instead. Beard, not bread, slipped down into the aperture. There was a flash, a bang and a crackle, and everything went dark. Zak threw himself under the table.

"It's the end of the world!" he cried. "Oh, help! Save us, Mr Jupiter! I don't want to die! I'm too young! I haven't even been to any other planets yet! Oh no! It really is the end of the world!"

"I don't think so, Zak," came Mr Jupiter's voice in the blackness. "I think it's just the end of my beard."

There was a slightly singed smell.

"I think you've blown a fuse," said China, groping her way to the window. "The whole street's gone dark...I can't see a light anywhere."

"It *is* the end of the world!" moaned Zak. "I knew it!"

"Don't be stupid, Zak," said China. "It's just a huge power failure. The whole city's gone dark. It's fantastic. Come and look!"

"There I go again," whimpered Mr Jupiter. "I can't stand the responsibility, I really can't. I can't even keep my beard under control, let alone everything else."

The power cut was enormous. The whole city was plunged into the dark – except hospitals and places that had their own generators.

"Goddamit!" cursed Nick, "a power cut."

"So bang goes our video game," grumbled Div. "I'd just got my finger on the button, too. Sickening! I wanted to see what it was like. Earth Destruct. Sounds amazing."

"Shut up," said Nick. "You got a match?"

Div lit one. In its brief flare of light, Nick

looked around.

"Better unplug it," he said. "It could be dangerous if the power comes back on and we're not here."

So Div unplugged the Earth Destruct machine.

"Are we going out, then?" he asked. "Shall we go for a drink?"

"It'll be dark there, too, you idiot," said Nick. And then he noticed something. "Hey, Div! There's a machine here – look, it's kind of glowing."

Div looked. It was true. One of Mr Jupiter's machines was faintly lit up. All the dials were glimmering in the dark, despite the power cut.

"It must have a battery."

"Yeah. Look – it's got a name on the top. What's it say?"

Reading was never Div's strong point, so Nick squinted at the illuminated sign.

"It says Ten Years Ahead."

"Let's have a go on it, eh? See what it does."

"We might as well," said Nick. "There's nothing else we can do till the lights come on." He fumbled with the machine until he found the starter button and pressed it. Immediately some strange electronic music started up.

"Hey!" breathed Div. "Weird!"

Then the machine spoke – or at least, a recorded voice did.

"Ten Years Ahead has much pleasure in presenting a scene from your very own future," it announced. "Please press button B." Nick obeyed. Immediately, a screen lit up. It flickered for a second or two and then cleared. And Nick and Div were amazed at what they saw. There, on the screen, were their own selves – sitting facing each other, only separated by a glass window. They looked very different. Nick's face was thin and pale. He looked very unhappy. But Div was well-dressed, his hair neatly cut, and all his spots had gone.

"So, you've come to visit me again, Div," said the Nick on the screen. "I don't know why you bother."

"Yeah, well – why not?" smiled the new improved Div. "You're an old mate."

"How are you doing?" asked Nick.

"Just fine. I've got my own business now. Flooring, you know. Carpets, tiles and stuff."

"Doing well?"

"Great. Thinking of building a swimming pool. You can have a swim in it when you get out. How much longer you got in here?"

"Two and a half years."

"Sooner you than me."

"Have you seen Rose at all?"

"Yeah. She's married now, you know."

"I heard. To that music teacher."

"I would've thought she'd stand by you."

"She did, the first time. But then I had to go and do it again, didn't I? And get caught – again."

"Longer sentences each time, eh?"

"Precisely. I must be crazy."

"Still, it's not long to go, is it? Before you get out."

"It seems like a lifetime when you're in here. And I've lost everything I cared about."

"Cheer up, Nick. Things can only get better, mate."

"I'm not sure."

Nick started to cough, the picture began to jump, and then the screen went blank.

For a moment or two, Nick and Div sat silent, too stunned to speak.

"Was that your idea of a joke, Div?" Nick asked.

"Are you kidding?" gawped Div. "Could I have organised a joke like that? You know how stupid

I am."

"Well, how was it done? It was us. Our voices and everything."

"It gives me the creeps," said Div, shuddering.

"I'd like to know who did it," muttered Nick. "And how they did it, too." They fell silent, thinking about what they had just seen. Fortune-telling was one thing but this was a whole different business. They had seen themselves – as they might be in ten years' time. Or was it as they *would* be?

"Not much of a future to look forward to, have you, Nick?"

"Any more remarks like that and you'll lose a few of your teeth, my friend," snapped Nick.

"Sorry, sorry," said Div. "Only joking. I thought that's what it all was, anyway. A practical joke."

"Funny kind of joke." Nick's voice sounded strange in the dark. Div wished he could see his face.

"What are we going to do this evening, anyway?" he asked, trying to get back to normal. "Are we just going to sit here in the dark?"

"Just sit here in the dark," confirmed Nick.

"And think."

Div sighed. He never had been much good at thinking. But Nick needed peace and quiet. Because Nick had a lot to think about.

# 21

Nick was glad it was dark in Div's room. He wouldn't want Div to see him shaking. The trembling went so deep, it felt as if a pneumatic drill was driving into his very heart and soul.

"Goddammit!" he thought. "It can't be true! Why should I let it get to me like this? It's just a stupid joke, somebody's kidding us along. Why should I let it bug me?"

Nick tried to whistle a tune to show how relaxed he was. The tune was an old classic called *Walk Like a Man*. But the way Nick whistled it, it didn't sound like that. It came out like *Crawl Like a Worm*.

That's what he felt like – a worm. It wasn't the first time he'd felt that way, either. Practically the whole of his childhood could more accurately be described as wormhood. Some days he'd felt so wormlike, he was scared of ending up as a blackbird's breakfast. Breakfast...breakfast... His memory played with the word.

"Yah, Nick Malin!" jeered a fat boy called Carl, out in the yard of the children's home. "Think you're tough? I'll have you for breakfast!"

And he had. Nick still had scars from the beatings-up he'd got there, and not just from Carl, either. Nick had been small for his age and some of the worst boys had treated him like a punch-bag.

"Right," he'd vowed one day, nursing a split lip, "I hate the lot of you. And one day I'm going to get my own back. You wait and see."

Nick realised now that he'd spent most of his life feeling mad at people. People who didn't deserve it as well as people who did. Hate, hate, hate. That's what had kept him going. Hate can be a lot more nourishing than a chocolate bar. It can give you the strength of ten men – really bad ones, though.

For as long as he could remember he'd wanted to score off people. To get to the top of the tree. To show them he was as good as they were – and better. Cleverer, tougher, and richer. What else was there to aim for? But now maybe he was beginning to feel there was something else after all. Because right now he didn't hate anyone quite so much as he hated himself.

And why? A girl's face came into his mind's eye. A pretty face, but covered with tears. It was a sight he was going to be seeing for real, all too soon. It was Rose's face. Nick realised that, for the first time in his life, he really cared about someone else. So much that it hurt.

I don't believe it! he thought, I'm in love!

Somehow Nick got the feeling he was never going to be much of a tough guy again.

Rose was different from all the other girls he'd known. She was pretty, like lots of others. And in a way, she was dumb, covering her pretty face with all that paint. But that was just the fashion. She'd grow out of it. What Nick liked about her was her odd mixture. Kind heart and fiery temper. One minute she'd be running her fingers through your hair, the next minute she'd be pulling it out by the handful.

She was a tender-hearted creature, too – sometimes the sight of a butcher's shop would make her cry for hours.

"Poor sheep!" she'd sob. "Poor cows! Why should they die for us? Why can't we eat beans instead?"

Nick grinned to himself in the dark.

What he liked most about Rose, though, was her loyalty. She was loyal to him, no matter how many times he stood her up, or teased her. And she was loyal to her family. She worried about her mum's business, or her dad being unemployed. And no matter how obnoxious her kid sister, China, was, Rose would leap to her defence.

"Oh my God!" she'd sighed, once. "Look at the mess China's made in here! Silver paper and scissors all over the floor! She really makes me sick sometimes!"

"Yeah," Nick had agreed. "She's too clever for her own good, that kid. A real bighead."

And Rose had turned on him.

"Don't you dare say things like that about China!"

Nick smiled to himself again.

If only he'd had a family like that, to fight with and be loyal to, then maybe he wouldn't feel so bad inside. Maybe he wouldn't need to be clever and superior, and cheat on people if he possibly could.

He wouldn't have had to prove that he wasn't good for nothing.

He felt really jealous of Rose's family. And yet why should he feel jealous? After all, they'd almost accepted him as one of them. In fact…if things had gone well, he might have ended up a member of that family, for real.

And now he'd completely blown it. He'd thrown away his chance. He felt so bad now, that he knew what he had to do. There was only one way to end the pain. It was so awful, he couldn't bear to think about it. And it would mean the end of everything, of course. But it had to be done. Nick stumbled to his feet.

"I'm going out, Div," he muttered. "Alone."

## 22

Rose was tidying up her room. Actually, it was tidy already, but she had a strange kind of knotted feeling inside, and the only way she could deal with it was by tidying. She looked enviously across at China's half of the room – the mountains of clothes, the jumble of junk. Her fingers itched to get to grips with that lot and give it the tidying-up of a lifetime.

But she knew it was not allowed. To China it would be interfering, messing about with her things. And strangely enough, despite the mess, China seemed to know exactly where everything was. So Rose sighed and rearranged her cosmetics bottles again, and polished them all until they were sparkling and clean. But it still didn't make her feel any better.

She leaned her forehead against the window

pane. Where had this depressed feeling come from? She knew all too well. It was ever since China had accused Nick of being a thief. Rose groaned. If only China could be friends with Nick. If only she could appreciate how great he was, what a joker, the life and soul of the party. But China was so stubborn, and lately, she had been getting such weird ideas. Rose was quite worried about her. She felt torn in half whenever China and Nick were in the same room, scared of what they'd say or do to each other.

Rose wondered what it would be like to be China. So carefree, so wild, with her secret friends and her superstitions and her love of mystery. Rose didn't like being herself, sometimes. Especially when she felt low. She stared gloomily at the street. And then, all of a sudden, Nick's car appeared and drew up outside the house. Rose jumped down from the window. Great! Nick would cheer her up, better than anybody. And luckily Staff was out with China. Staff had never really got over his suspicions of Nick.

Rose ran to the door and opened it before Nick had time to ring.

"Nick! Fantastic to see you! Everyone's out

except me, and I was getting a bit low. What's the matter?"

She'd never seen Nick look so serious. His face seemed almost a different shape.

"I got to tell you something, Rose," he said gravely, and they sat down together on the sofa. Rose's pulse was beating wildly.

"I know what it is!" she cried, in an agony of anticipation. "It's another girl, isn't it? You've met somebody new. You want to finish with me. I know. I can tell."

Nick stared at her in amazement, then gave a weak little laugh. He grabbed her hand and squeezed it tight.

"You're mad, girl," he whispered. "You're the best thing in my life – OK?"

He looked so desperate, Rose was astonished. He'd never talked like that before. What was wrong?

"What is it? Oh, what is it?" she asked. Nick dropped his head into his hands.

"I did something…stupid, Rose."

"What? What?"

"It was me – I broke into your mum's place and stole all that stuff."

"But Nick! You aren't kidding, are you? Oh Nick – for heaven's sake – why?"

Nick leaned back and sighed deeply.

"I don't know. I…well, the first thing is, I was short of money."

"Can't you manage on your wages? I thought you were doing well."

"I…you…I never told you, Rose, but I lost my job a couple of months ago."

"Nick! Why?"

Rose dreaded the reason. Had Nick been dishonest there, too?

"The business went bust. Honestly. Believe me, Rose."

Rose stared at him in amazement, trying to come to terms with what she was hearing.

"Well, since then, I've been pretty broke. And I wanted to take you out – give you a good time."

"So you decided to steal from my mum," flashed Rose in a sudden burst of rage.

"That's…well, that's how it must seem, sure. But you see, I…I knew it would be easy, and I knew she was insured. I was here that time they were discussing the money angle, remember?

And I knew that nobody could get hurt."

"Oh, so that makes it all right, does it?" said Rose, trying to control her temper.

"No, no, of course not, Rose. Nothing could make it all right." Nick dropped his head into his hands again. "I've been going wrong for ages now. I don't know why. I feel so angry inside."

Rose laid her hand timidly on his shoulder.

"Poor Nick."

"There's more yet, Rose."

"More?"

"Div and I raided Mr Jupiter's place this morning."

"Oh, Nick!"

"It was the last time – honest, Rose – and I'll never do anything like that again."

"But Nick, what are we going to do about it?"

Nick looked up at her.

"Did you say, we?"

"Yes, of course. What are we going to do?"

"You mean – you'll stand by me, Rose?"

"Of course."

"I thought you'd want to finish with me for good."

Rose stared at him. For the first time, Nick really seemed to need her. Instead of waiting for him to ring, and praying he wouldn't meet someone else, now she had things to do. She had to think fast, to organise things, to talk to people, to speak up for him. Suddenly, Rose's life seemed full of important things to do – real challenges. In a curious way, despite what Nick had told her, Rose felt better than she'd felt for ages. Her heart was lighter and lighter.

"I'll go and make a cup of tea," she said. "That's what Mum always does in emergencies." And she got up. But Nick seized her hand as she passed.

"Rose, do you mean…" He stared up at her. "Do you really mean it – that you'd stand by me and help me and all?"

"Of course," said Rose quietly. "I rather like you, you know."

And Nick, acting on impulse, suddenly turned into an old-fashioned knight, and kissed his lady's hand.

# 23

"My parents won't be home till late," said Rose, as they sipped their tea. "It's their wedding anniversary."

"Oh no!" groaned Nick. "It'll really spoil their day when they find out. I can't face telling them. Will you help me, Rose?"

Rose squeezed his hand. She felt equal to anything at the moment. And she was sure her parents would forgive Nick in the end. They had to. Nick badly needed some help and support if he was going to make a new start. And if he didn't make a new start now, Rose was sure he never would.

"The first thing we have to do, though," said Nick, "is take all that stuff back to Mr Jupiter's. Will you give me a hand, Rose?"

"Of course," said Rose.

"The stuff's all very dusty, though," said Nick.

"Maybe you'd better change your clothes."

Rose ran off to her room and reappeared wearing a sweater, jeans and running shoes.

"I haven't worn anything like this for ages," she grinned, and skipped around the sofa. "I feel like a kid again. This is what it must be like to be China."

"Oh no!" said Nick. "China! She'll eat me alive! She never liked me. And she's so crazy about Mr Jupiter."

"Hey!" smiled Rose, "I thought you were a Big Shot! Don't tell me you're afraid of my little sister!"

"Who isn't? She's some kid!" said Nick. "She's always seen right through me, that's why. Eyes like lasers."

"Come on," said Rose, "let's go!"

Nick drove her round to Div's, where the van was still parked in a little side alley.

"Right, Div," instructed Nick. "We're going to load up all this stuff back in the van."

"Thank God for that," said Div. "I can't move in here. And besides, it gives me the creeps, this stuff. Where are we taking it?"

"Back to the old man."

Div stared in astonishment.

"You had second thoughts, then?"

"Second, third and fourth thoughts."

It took quite a long time to load the van, but at last every last fragment was picked up off Div's disgusting carpet – every screw, every button.

"Right," said Nick. "Now we take it back. Are you coming, Div?"

Div shook his head. "It makes me feel bad," he said. "Tying up that poor old guy, you know. I'll never forget the look in his eyes."

"Well, come along with us and tell him you're sorry, then."

"No. I can't. You do it for me. There was something about him – I don't know – I can't face him. I feel more like hiding from him to tell you the truth."

So Div went back inside the tenement and Nick drove off to Mr Jupiter's with Rose at his side.

"I've never met this Mr Jupiter," she said. "I'm quite curious to see what he's like."

"Oh, he's just a funny little old guy with a long white beard," said Nick. "But all the same, he certainly has a way with machines." And he told Rose about the machine, and the vision it

118

had given him of what was in store.

"You married a music teacher," said Nick.

"Well, you watch your step, Nick Malin," smiled Rose. "Or I might just do that. I've always been very fond of music."

"I have to ask Mr Jupiter about it," said Nick. "I mean, is that my future, no matter what? If I'm destined to go to jail, what point is there in trying to make a new start?"

"Come on," insisted Rose, "you're making that new start, Nick Malin, come what may."

But deep inside she felt a quiver of uncertainty. Was Nick really going to give up his bad ways? Only time would tell.

# 24

"You really must go home, children," said Mr Jupiter. "The power's been back on for an hour and a half now. And so far the world hasn't ended. I think we're all right."

"I'd rather stay here," said Zak. "Suppose the world ends in the middle of the night when I'm asleep? I wouldn't be able to do anything about it."

"Don't be stupid, Zak," said China. "What could you do anyway?"

"At least if we were here, with Mr Jupiter, he could beam us off to another galaxy."

"I've told you before, Zak – I can't do any such thing."

"Can't you save us, then?"

"It's not a question of saving you." Mr Jupiter began to look exasperated. "There are some things which…must remain a mystery. But China – you really ought to go, you know. It's getting late."

China seemed reluctant to go, too.

"It's OK," she said. "It's my parents' wedding anniversary and they're having a night out."

"What's bothering you, my dear?" enquired Mr Jupiter. "I can see something's the matter. Now speak up!"

"It's Nick," confessed China. "Ever since I heard him on that machine of yours saying he was going to fit us with silencers – permanently – I've been really, really scared. And now Rose knows that I suspect Nick, she's bound to tell him. And then – well, I'm sure he's going to get me."

"That's not like you, China, to be so nervous," Mr Jupiter said.

"But why shouldn't I be scared, Mr Jupiter? You're terrified out of your wits half the time, and you're a—"

"Never mind about me." Mr Jupiter smiled. "I'm just a feeble old man. But I depend on you, China, to show some courage. Fight the good fight, you know. Now, you really must run along home."

"We could telephone our parents," said Zak,

"and tell them where we are."

"Telephones?" muttered Mr Jupiter. "Nasty modern inventions. Never could get along with them – never had one in the house. Now, really, you two, I must insist – you must go home. You are in absolutely no danger, I assure you."

Just then, Mr Jupiter's doorbell rang, with a strange sudden burst of sound. *Jangle, jangle!* China almost jumped out of her skin.

"Dear me," said Mr Jupiter. "Whoever can that be, at this time of night? I don't think I'd better answer it."

They all stood stock still, not daring to breathe. Then the bell rang again, and a heavy fist pounded at the door.

"They've seen the light," whispered China. "They know we're here."

Mr Jupiter hesitated. He plaited his beard into a dozen knots.

"Mr Jupiter!" called a voice outside. "Open the door! We've got something for you."

"It's Nick!" hissed China, and her blood froze. Mr Jupiter went pale.

"I must..." he muttered, "I must...try and

face them, somehow. Come, children!"

Mr Jupiter flip-flopped in his slippers to the door, and China and Zak followed behind. China grabbed Mr Jupiter's broken old tennis racket as she went – just in case she had to defend him. Through the frosted glass of the front door they could see two vague shapes. Mr Jupiter struggled with the locks and bolts, the door swung open, and there stood Rose – and Nick! China shrieked aloud.

"She's told him!" screamed China. "He's come for me!"

"Take it easy, China," said Nick. "I won't hurt you."

"It's true, China," added Rose. "Nick's not going to hurt anybody."

"But he said he was going to fit us with silencers!"

Nick looked amazed.

"How did you know that?"

"I heard it – on one of Mr Jupiter's machines!"

Mr Jupiter groaned.

"I was only kidding, China," said Nick. "And it's all over, anyway, now. I'm going straight from now on."

"You were right, China," said Rose. "Nick did do

the robbery on Mum's place. He confessed everything to me. And he wants to put it all right."

"Well done, well done, young man!" said Mr Jupiter, beaming. "How rarely, nowadays, one hears anything at all about regret, remorse, and so on. Come in, come in."

Nick and Rose stepped inside.

"I've brought all your machines back, Mr Jupiter," said Nick. "I'm really sorry for what I did. Will you, you know…forgive me?"

"Forgive you, my dear young man? It'll be a pleasure!" Mr Jupiter was wreathed in smiles. Nick turned to China.

"And you, China," he said. "You saw through me all along. You never liked me, did you?"

China wriggled uncomfortably.

"Not much," she admitted.

"Don't be too hard on me, kid," said Nick. "I'm going to make a new start. And it'll be a great day for me when I can count China Lee as my friend."

China blushed and looked at the floor.

"What about all Mum's stuff?" she asked. "Are you going to give that back, too?"

"I can't," said Nick. "I sold it. But I'll pay her

back, every penny. I'll go to the police and tell 'em everything. Give them the works. And I'll take my punishment."

"Quite right, quite right," murmured Mr Jupiter. "Maybe sooner or later your mum and dad will forgive me, too."

"Will he go to prison, Mr Jupiter?" asked China.

Mr Jupiter wrinkled his brow and scratched his head.

"I – I can hardly say, my dear," he said. "Two burglaries – no, you needn't mention mine – in fact, I'd be obliged if you absolutely wouldn't – one burglary, then, and a very penitent attitude on the young man's part...the desire to make a new start, and so on...if I were the one to judge, I would be inclined to forgive and forget, you know. Although some punishment is in order, of course. Oh dear, I get so muddled about this. Perhaps you will be put on...what's it called? Probity?"

"Probation," said Nick. "Do you really think I can get away with probation?"

"I have nothing to do with the legal system," said Mr Jupiter. "I can't guarantee anything. But you mustn't think of it as getting away with anything. That's the old Nick talking."

Nick nodded.

"Have you brought back the Earth Destruct machine?" asked Zak nervously.

"Yeah," said Nick. "They're all out in the van. Everything's there. Oh – and my mate would like to apologise to you, too, Mr Jupiter."

"Ah," murmured Mr Jupiter, stroking his beard dreamily, "Div has had a change of heart, too, has he? Good, good! I'm worried about that young man…"

"How did you know he was called Div?" asked Nick in amazement.

Mr Jupiter got confused.

"Ah – oh, I…er, I expect China told me!"

China said nothing, only she felt an odd thrill of wonder. She hadn't known Nick's friend was called Div.

"Nick…" said Zak. "Couldn't you bring the Earth Destruct machine in? Someone might steal the van."

"Sure – in a minute," said Nick. "I just wanted to ask Mr Jupiter about one of his machines. The Ten Years Ahead machine."

Mr Jupiter looked worried.

"We had a go on it," explained Nick. "And it showed a scene from our future. Does that mean it's bound to happen? I mean, whatever we do?"

Mr Jupiter went pink.

"It's not – not exactly certain," he said. "That's to say – the machine has always been very unreliable."

"But," Nick said, "if it showed you something bad that was going to happen to you, is that it? I mean, are we, you know – what's the word?"

"Pre-destined?" corrected Mr Jupiter. "People have argued about this for centuries, haven't they? And I'm sure my poor old head is too muddled to throw any light on the subject. All I can say is, as to the machine…it gives a reading according to the state of mind of the enquirer, at the moment the machine is used. The result can vary if the state of mind changes."

"Eh?" said Zak, gawping.

"It's easy, Zak," explained China. "If you had a go on the machine in one of your greedy moods, it would say that you were destined to become very fat, but if you were on a diet, then it would say that you'd be slim – isn't that right, Mr Jupiter?"

"I think so, China," said Mr Jupiter. "Something like that, anyway."

"Well, let's hope so," murmured Nick. "It's my only hope."

"Cling to your hope, young man," said Mr Jupiter. "It will see you through your darkest hour."

"Couldn't we get the Earth Destruct machine in now, please?" asked Zak. "And maybe Mr Jupiter could dismantle it. Make it safe."

They carried all Mr Jupiter's machines back into the workshop. Mr Jupiter beamed to see them, and tottered about fiddling with them like a little boy at Christmas with a stocking full of new toys.

"That's the lot, Mr Jupiter," said Nick. "But before we go, I'd really like to talk to you about how you make your machines."

Mr Jupiter looked nervous.

"Ah – I, er, I tell you what, Nick," he said. "It's long past my bedtime, and I've had a tiring day. Come back tomorrow and we'll talk about it. And now be so good as to take these children safely home, will you?"

"Right you are, Mr Jupiter," said Nick. "See you tomorrow, then."

"Of course, of course," smiled Mr Jupiter. "I'll never forget your kindness to me today – all of you. Goodnight, China, my dear!" And for a moment, he gave China a special kind of look, that seemed to go right through her, and made her feel warm and safe.

"Goodnight, Mr Jupiter," said China. "And take care."

# 25

"What an amazing old guy," said Nick, as they drove home.

"China's mad about him, aren't you, China?" said Rose. "She thinks the world of him."

China said nothing. But she was proud that Mr Jupiter was her own very special friend.

"China reckons that Mr Jupiter is a god!" Zak burst out.

"Shut up, Zak!" hissed China, in alarm.

"A god?" asked Rose. "Don't be stupid! There aren't any gods. Honestly, China!"

"She reckons," Zak went on, "that Mr Jupiter is a god sort of secretly living among us, and his machines are his ways of controlling the world."

"What garbage, Zak!" laughed Rose. "You've been reading too much science fiction! Surely you don't believe all this, China?"

"Shut up, Zak," said China. "I don't want to talk about it. Don't you remember – we promised."

But Zak was in such a state, after the excitements of the day, that he couldn't be stopped.

"But lots of really weird things have happened," he said. "First, Mr Jupiter had a flood in his kitchen and the next day it rained and rained and there were floods all over the country, and then when he got his beard caught in the toaster there was this huge enormous power cut over the entire whole city—"

"Come on, Zak," laughed Rose. "You're just being—"

"No, Rose, let him go on," interrupted Nick, who had been strangely silent so far. "Give me the works, Zak. Fill me in."

"Well, his machines are all pretty amazing," said Zak. China's heart sank as he rattled on. Soon, poor Mr Jupiter would have no secrets left. "He had this machine that could listen in to anybody's house, anywhere, and one that could find lost dogs, and one that could show you what happened yesterday – anywhere and to anybody."

"And the Ten Years Ahead machine," added Nick. "That was incredible, Rose."

"And most of all," Zak went on, "there's this one called Earth Destruct – you only have to press the button and the whole Earth goes up in smoke – BANG – and that's the end of everything."

"Wow!" said Nick, going pale.

"I hope he'll dismantle that one," said Zak, biting his nails. "But anyway – what he said was, he had to have a machine in case everything went wrong in the world and he had to destroy it all and start all over again."

"I don't suppose he really said that, Zak," said Rose. "You're just getting carried away with the excitement of it all."

"No – he did, he really and truly did, didn't he, China?"

China refused to answer. She would certainly never trust Zak with a secret again.

"I mean, only a god would say that kind of thing! Wouldn't he?" persisted Zak.

"I think he's just a slightly crazy old man," said Rose. "How can he be a god? Living in a dump like that. And anyway – how can there be any gods at all

– on Earth or anywhere else?"

"What do you mean?" asked Zak.

"Well, the world's in such a mess," Rose explained. "All the wars and violence and the famines and things. And all the disease and crimes and everything. How can there be a god?"

"If God was a feeble old man in a muddle," China suddenly burst out, "it would explain everything. He was always going on about how everything was out of control, and how he couldn't cope. Maybe he can still manage the odd miracle with his machines, but – oh, never mind."

The van drew up outside the Lees' home. There were still no lights on. Evidently their parents were still out celebrating their wedding anniversary.

"Look," said Nick. "I won't stay and tell your mum and dad tonight. It's too late, and I don't want to spoil things for 'em. I'll come round tomorrow – we'll tell them then, and then I'll go round to the police station."

"Oh yeah?" said China. "How do we know you're not going to disappear in the night? Run away and never come back?"

"I know I deserve that, China," said Nick, with

the sad ghost of a grin, "but I'll just have to ask you to trust me. And anyway, there's something I want to do first tomorrow. Before I tell your parents."

"What?"

"I want to go round and see Mr Jupiter again. Everything Zak's been saying may sound far-fetched, but there's something about that old guy that's kind of – well, he made a strange impression on me."

"I don't think we should bother him!" said China, trying to head Nick off.

"I don't want to be any trouble. I just want to ask him a few questions," said Nick. "I mean, it'd be incredible if…you know."

"I think we should leave him alone," insisted China.

"Yeah – but think of the reaction, China. Think what the newspapers and the TV would make of it," said Nick. "It'd be the biggest story of all time."

"Yeah!" put in Zak. "Mr Jupiter could get to be a TV star. He could probably have his own chat show and everything. He wouldn't have to live in a crummy little house like that any more."

China shuddered.

"But—"

"It really is sad that a guy as important and clever as him – whatever he is has – to live in such a state," Nick went on.

"Yes!" added Zak. "I mean, he could be a megastar!"

"No, no!" said China. "He wouldn't like that at all."

"We'll see," said Nick. "Let's all go and see him tomorrow morning, first thing. It's my last request, China – as a condemned man. Remember, I'm going to give myself up right afterwards."

China shrugged. She knew it was useless to argue. But she was so worried about what might happen that she hardly got a wink of sleep all night.

"Please, God," she whispered. "Or should I say Mr— oh dear, it's all so confusing. But anyway, please, please…make it all right."

# 26

Next morning, China felt terrible. She'd slept so badly she was quite pale and shaky. What would Nick say to Mr Jupiter? Would he upset him dreadfully? Would Mr Jupiter get really angry so his eyes flashed, like he did once before? Would Zak say something utterly stupid? She was so tense she couldn't face any breakfast at all.

"I'm going to see Mr Jupiter," she announced, pulling on her jacket. "C'mon, Staff!"

"I'm coming, too," said Rose.

Oh no, thought China. This is getting worse by the minute. If Rose starts to go on about how there can't be any gods, because the world is in such a terrible state – I shall die of shame.

"So…Mr Jupiter is certainly getting popular," said Mum. "I hope you girls aren't making nuisances of yourselves."

"No, Mum!" said China. "We just – you know – help him and stuff."

Though as she shot out of the door, with Staff at her heels, she couldn't help thinking how it was really Mr Jupiter who had helped her – again and again. She'd never done anything to help him. But today she really must. Mr Jupiter must be allowed to keep his secrets, to guard his mystery, and live as he liked, whatever happened.

They'd agreed to meet Nick and Zak by the bandstand in the park.

"There's Nick!" said Rose. "I told you he would show up, China. He's really changed, you know." But Rose was secretly relieved.

"I hope so," said China. "I just wish I could believe it."

"Even Staff believes it," said Rose. "Didn't you notice yesterday? As soon as Nick confessed everything, Staff was all friendly to him again."

"Yes, I noticed," admitted China. "I just wish Nick wouldn't bother Mr Jupiter like this."

"Don't be silly, China. Mr Jupiter actually asked Nick to come back today – remember? He's probably expecting us. I'm sure he won't mind."

China wasn't so sure. She was desperately sorry that she and Zak hadn't kept their promise to Mr Jupiter. They should never have said anything about him – to anybody. But then – if China had never told anyone anything about Mr Jupiter, Nick would never have had his change of heart. Things were very confusing.

"You must be very gentle with him, Nick," said Rose as they walked towards Lordship Road. "China's worried that you'll upset him."

"I promise I won't upset the old guy, China," said Nick. "I just want to ask him how he made his machines, you know – just get some idea of what he's really all about."

China said nothing. She didn't think it was at all wise to try and get some idea of what Mr Jupiter was all about. But it was too late now. They were already turning into Mr Jupiter's street.

Please, please, Mr God— China thought desperately (she was getting more than a little muddled), make it all right. If you make it all right, I promise to keep my bedroom tidy forever and ever amen.

Now they were almost at Mr Jupiter's house. But wait! What was this? Some men were in the front garden with ladders and scaffolding poles.

"Hey," cried China. "Where's Mr Jupiter?"

"What?" asked the men. "Who?"

"Mr Jupiter," insisted China. "He lives here. An old man with a white beard."

"Sounds like Santa Claus," said the tall man, and the other one laughed.

"Nobody's lived here for years, sweetheart," said the taller man. "The place has been locked up since the old lady died who owned it – when was that, Charley?"

"A coupla years ago, at least."

"But—" China scrambled over the oil drums in the front garden and peeped in through the windows. What had been Mr Jupiter's workshop was empty – completely cleared.

"He's gone," she said, and felt a wave of relief and sadness at the same time. Staff whimpered slightly, and a breeze sprang up.

"But we saw him only yesterday," said Nick. "Last night he was here. Have all his machines gone, China?"

"Yes," said China, relaxed at last. Mr Jupiter was safe, thank heaven. "See for yourself, Nick."

Nick peered through the window.

"Are you sure?" he asked the men. "Are you certain no one's lived here recently?"

"Sure, I'm sure," said the short man. "I live just down the road. There ain't been nobody near the place for years. It's been boarded up. The City Council's bought the place, now, and we've come to renovate it."

"But – where have the machines gone?"

"Machines? There weren't no machines. Nothin' but a few odds and ends – and they're all over there in the skip." The man pointed to a huge bin out in the road, where a mattress and a few sticks of furniture lay.

"Oh, there's his toaster," cried China, and ran and picked it up. "Please may I keep it?"

"Of course you can, sweetheart. It's only going off to the dump."

Zak peered into the skip.

"None of his machines are here," he reported. "It's all gone. Vanished. I expect he's beamed it all off to another galaxy."

"Well," sighed Nick. "That's the weirdest thing I ever heard. But he really has gone. Ah well. I suppose I'd better be going back to your parents' place, Rose. I have to tell them all about the real me, and then go to the police. I'm dreading it."

"It'll be all right," said Rose, taking his hand. "I'll stand by you. Are you coming, China?"

"I think I'll just hang about here for a while," said China.

So Nick and Rose went off to face whatever fate had in store for them, while China and Zak sat on Mr Jupiter's wall for a while and kicked their heels.

"We didn't imagine it, did we, China?" asked Zak.

"Of course not! This is his toaster, isn't it?"

"Can I…have a look at it?"

"All right, but don't touch! It's mine!"

"OK – I just thought there might be a bit of burnt beard inside it. To sort of – prove it, if you know what I mean."

There wasn't, though. Only a few black crumbs.

"I don't need proof," said China. "I know what I think, and I'm sure I'm right about this, if nothing else." And she hugged the toaster so tight, Staff got a little bit jealous.

Later that day, China tidied her room up, just like she had promised in her prayer. She found all sorts of things she thought she'd lost. And she also discovered that her side of the room was a lot bigger when all her clothes were safely folded away. Big enough to have some really good fights in, in the future.

"Goodness!" said Rose, peering round the door, "Whatever's happened in here? Are you feeling all right, China?"

"I'm tidying it up for Mr Jupiter," said China awkwardly. "To sort of…remember him by."

"Well, that just shows how crazy you are," said Rose. "Mr Jupiter was the untidiest old man I've ever seen."

China thought about that a bit. Rose had a point. But she liked it this way, all the same.

China took her toaster and placed it right in the middle of her top shelf, in place of honour between the secret diary and the stickers book. And there it stayed, forever afterwards – the toaster that saved the world.

"You see, I tidied up, Mr," whispered China. "You don't mind if I call you Mr from now on, do you?

Only God is such a frightening kind of word, and I think I know now that you're not really frightening at all.

"Anyway, thanks a million for making it all right. And I hope you're OK now, wherever you are. I wish you could've stayed, but I know you had to go. But I just wanted to say that I'm really really going to miss you. Goodbye Mr and amen."

# More Orchard Red Apples

All priced at £4.99

Orchard Red Apples are available from all good bookshops,
or can be ordered direct from the publisher:
Orchard Books, PO BOX 29, Douglas IM99 1BQ
Credit card orders please telephone 01624 836000
or fax 01624 837033
or visit our Internet site: www.wattspub.co.uk
or e-mail: bookshop@enterprise.net for details.

To order please quote title, author and ISBN
and your full name and address.
Cheques and postal orders should be made payable to 'Bookpost plc.'
Postage and packing is FREE within the UK
(overseas customers should add £1.00 per book)

Prices and availability are subject to change.